# SPECIAL MESSAGE TO READERS

## THE ULVERSCROFT FOUNDATION
**(registered UK charity number 264873)**
was established in 1972 to provide funds for research, diagnosis and treatment of eye diseases.
Examples of major projects funded by the Ulverscroft Foundation are:-

- The Children's Eye Unit at Moorfields Eye Hospital, London
- The Ulverscroft Children's Eye Unit at Great Ormond Street Hospital for Sick Children
- Funding research into eye diseases and treatment at the Department of Ophthalmology, University of Leicester
- The Ulverscroft Vision Research Group, Institute of Child Health
- Twin operating theatres at the Western Ophthalmic Hospital, London
- The Chair of Ophthalmology at the Royal Australian College of Ophthalmologists

You can help further the work of the Foundation by making a donation or leaving a legacy.
Every contribution is gratefully received. If you would like to help support the Foundation or require further information, please contact:

**THE ULVERSCROFT FOUNDATION**
**The Green, Bradgate Road, Anstey**
**Leicester LE7 7FU, England**
**Tel: (0116) 236 4325**

**website: www.foundation.ulverscroft.com**

# SURGEON IN PORTUGAL

'A strong dose of sunshine' is the prescription for Nurse Liz Larking, recovering from glandular fever. And a villa in the Algarve seems the ideal place to recuperate, even if it means cooking for the villa's owner, eminent cardiac surgeon Hugh Forsythe: brilliant, caring, awe-inspiring — and dangerously easy to fall in love with. Liz soon realises that this doctor is more potent than any virus — and ironically, it seems he could just as easily break a heart as cure one . . .

Books by Anna Ramsay
in the Linford Romance Library:

MISTLETOE MEDICINE
HEARTBEAT

ANNA RAMSAY

# SURGEON IN PORTUGAL

*Complete and Unabridged*

LINFORD
*Leicester*

First published in Great Britain in 1986

First Linford Edition
published 2014

A catalogue record for this book is available
from the British Library.

ISBN 978–1–4448–1866–6

Published by
F. A. Thorpe (Publishing)
Anstey, Leicestershire

Set by Words & Graphics Ltd.
Anstey, Leicestershire
Printed and bound in Great Britain by
T. J. International Ltd., Padstow, Cornwall

This book is printed on acid-free paper

# 1

Dr Paul Larking moved with stealthy care to where Liz lay sleeping, his footsteps drowned in a sea of green Wilton. The fever was past. Her temperature must be back to normal; this was deep and health-giving slumber. Paul checked his watch. She'd lain there for hours, never moving, her breathing slow and even.

He watched his sister in silence, still as a statue himself.

The girl's face, cushioned against blue and pink glazed chintz roses, was drained of colour and beneath the closed lids mauve shadows stood out like bruised thumb-prints on wax. Paul brooded over the possibility that she might be a bit anaemic, and wondered if her own GP was being vigilant about blood tests till her system was clear of the virus. Not that glandular fever was exactly a life-threatening illness . . .

What a struggle it must have meant for Liz! She'd said nothing, though, to anyone, till her nursing finals were over. Typical! Sticking stubbornly on her feet, right up until the virus surged to an acute stage of infection and she could fight it no longer. It must have taken a supreme effort of will, but she'd cracked it in spite of the glandular fever. Elizabeth Larking, fully qualified Nightingale. Wings clipped for the time being, to be sure.

Infectious mononucleosis — could persist for months, mused the doctor. Especially in young adults. And then, just when you believed you were over it — as Liz had — back came the fever as if to say, tricked you! You haven't got rid of me yet.

A log crackled in the fireplace and spat out a glowing spark on to the creamy stone of the hearth, breaking Paul's concentration. With a polished black toecap he stubbed out the red speck of fire and examined in the flickering light the groups of photo-graphs in their silver frames. Sentimental woman, his mother — all these pictures of him and Liz, right from the year dot. Big brother with a protective arm about tiny blonde sister. Medical student in graduation gown and mortarboard. Liz with a big smile on her face, fair hair scraped up under the cap of a first-year nurse. Dad, taken in the orchard about six weeks before he died.

Suddenly behind him the plaid rug heaved and a slight figure sat bolt upright, yawning and rubbing its eyes with childish fists. 'Whatever brings you home, brother dear? Have you been summoned for the post-mortem, then?'

Paul swung round in time to see his sister lowering bare toes to the floor and reaching for her dressing gown. 'Put your slippers on, Liz, or your feet will get cold. Do my eyes deceive me, or have you been losing weight? You've got legs like pea-sticks — '

'Huh, that'll be the day! I'm rather

proud of my new waistline, though. Get a load of this.' Liz pulled her belt tight about the white towelling robe and sucked in her cheeks in a glamorous pose, then padded over to her tall black-browed brother and stood on tiptoe to reach his lean cheek. 'I'm glad you've come, Paul. Only *you* can possibly convince our mother that with glandular fever the normal pattern is up one day, down the next. Wouldn't you expect,' she continued in her low, husky voice, 'that Mum would demonstrate a little more faith in her children's professional skills? Since Dad died she's got even worse. I only hope having Auntie Meg living here is going to make her less dependent on my being around.'

Paul's black brows drew together as he considered how Liz, ten years his junior, had been tied to Mrs Larking's apron strings. Their father, a local headmaster, had been forced through ill-health to take early retirement, and his wife had given up her part-time teaching post in the school's Home Economics department, to look after him. When David Larking had died, Liz was still in the Lower Sixth and Paul doing his surgical house job at the Royal Hanoverian Hospital in east London. Liz had been going to train there in the School of Nursing, but rather than leave her mother alone in the big house Mrs Larking refused to sell on account of its sentimental memories, she had trained locally at the General instead. After all, she'd pointed out with her usual cheerful optimism, one school of nursing is much the same as the next.

Hmm, thought Paul. She'd have had a lot more fun with him at the Royal Hanoverian. 'Throat better? Glands settled down?'

'Yes, yes, yes,' came the hasty reply.

'Got your appetite back?'

'No, thanks, I look much better without it! Has Mum told you the great news, that I *have* been awarded a place at the Hanoverian in September?'

'The specialist course in Intensive Care! That's terrific, Liz, it really is. We'll take you to all the parties, Pam and I, introduce you to lots of nice young doctors. We'll find you a husband before you know where you are.' Paul guarded his diaphragm against the unfriendly punch coming his way. The trouble with young sisters, they learned the hard way how to take care of themselves. Liz was still a bit of a tomboy, even after all these years.

'I can wait for that privilege. After all, it took you and Pam long enough to take the plunge. I haven't the time for *marriage*,' spluttered Liz disparagingly. 'Goodness, I've hardly had a boy-friend in the last three years! You try having any social life when Mother doesn't like being on her own after dark. All this wearisome organisation getting Auntie Meg to stay here when I've been on nights. No way, Paul, it's going to take me time enough getting used to living away from home. Pathetic, isn't it, at the ripe old age of twenty-two.'

Two spots of hectic colour had sprung up on Liz's cheekbones. Paul touched her forehead with the back of one hand, closed his fingers over her wrist, checking her pulse. Obediently Liz stood still, subduing the inner fount of excitement at this new stage in her life. You couldn't really expect Paul to understand how it felt to know that at *last* you'd be going to London, to that very hospital you'd dreamed of through your teenage years. It was an honour and a privilege to be given a place. Such courses for trained nurses, run by the Joint Board of Clinical Nursing Studies, were heavily over-subscribed.

With fond grey eyes Liz watched her brother's professional face. He was a physician, a registrar now, on the ladder leading to a consultancy. He looked just like Tom Conti! No wonder all the nurses had been after him. But six months ago he'd married a copper-headed physio named Pam, who couldn't even boil an egg. When her wrist was released Liz began pacing up and down, hands thrust deep into dressing-gown pockets, bottom lip out-thrust in one of these perplexing changes of mood that had been overtaking her lately. It must be the wretched glands.

'Paul — ' she questioned seriously, as her brother leaned an elbow on the fireplace and watched her restless movements. 'Paul, you are sure it isn't selfish of me, leaving home for more training instead of taking that staff job they've offered me at the General?'

'You must be joking! How many other girls would have been prepared to make the sacrifices you have?'

'Lots,' came the indignant response. 'It's ridiculous to talk about sacrifices when Mum needed me so badly. With her own sister now in the same boat, she doesn't need me any longer. Far better to live together in one house and sell the other. Say, isn't that Mum calling us for supper?'

Mrs Larking adored cooking. Liz was more into healthy eating, plenty of bran and roughage and uncooked fruit and veg. Even so, her mother's lovingly prepared delicacies were well-nigh irresistible, and with Paul home she'd really killed the fatted calf. 'What a pity Pam had to work this weekend,' she said as she spooned the creamy perfection of a spinach soufflé on to the Royal Doulton. 'Will that do you, Paul dear?'

Her son was eyeing the soufflé, soaring above its paper frill, golden-topped with a sprinkling of cheese and breadcrumbs. Pam had just cracked the art of the grilled fish finger. 'Wonderful! Perhaps just another couple of spoons . . .'

'Pam taken the L-plates off yet?' enquired Liz with a nonchalant grin.

'Really, dear!' reproved her mother. 'After the ardours of physiotherapy *I* certainly shouldn't want to spend hours in the kitchen over Paul's supper. And I shouldn't care to entrust our Sunday roast to *you* either.'

'Oh, lord!' observed Paul with unusual

concern, catching his mother's eye and pulling faces. 'Don't tell me Liz is a duff cook too.'

'It's *what* she cooks that I'm referring to. Roast lamb? Not a bit of it. Nut cutlets and muesli, that's what we'd be eating tonight if I left it to Miss Elizabeth here.'

'Lovely!' teased her daughter. 'But I do approve of this soufflé, it's absolutely delicious. What's the matter with you, Paul? Why do you keep trying to catch Mum's eye and giving her funny looks?'

Paul refused a third helping and rested his arms on the table, his expression portentous. 'Your mother and I have been discussing your convalescence,' he said severely, sounding just like Mr Larking in his head-masterly days. 'She feels, Liz, that you're making rather slow progress.'

'You'd think she was getting over an operation,' butted in Mrs Larking in a complaining tone. 'She was always such a good little eater.'

Liz raised her eyes to heaven and mouthed along with her brother's voice. 'After glandular fever, convalescence can be not unlike that required after surgery. Vitamins can be as helpful in those convalescing after a fever as after an operation. Liz needs a multi-vitamin preparation, and a strong dose of sunshine.'

'You'll be advising minced raw liver next!' muttered Liz, vexed by all this discussion of her state of health. Like most nurses she considered falling ill a nuisance, to be shaken off as fast as possible so she could get back to her rightful job of looking after others.

'And I've another recommendation,' went on Paul ominously.

'*Really*, doctor?' observed Liz sweetly. 'Let me just remind you of the ethics of prescribing for your own family?'

'Shut up, pest, and listen for a change. For an invalid you've far too much to say for yourself. Just hear me out.' Paul tilted the wine bottle over his mother's glass, but she pushed his hand aside.

'No more for me, dear, or I'll be under the table! You tell her about it now. Not that I don't have my reservations — you know how I feel about aeroplanes.'

Paul gave his mother one of those special smiles he generally kept for his most nervous patients. She got up and started to clear away the dishes and Liz automatically rose to help her.

'No, dear, I can manage. You sit there and listen to your brother. He seems to think it's a good idea for you to go flying off to Portugal for a couple of months. I'm sure I don't know . . . but if that sunshine's going to get you right for September, then never let it be said I stood in your way.'

That night Liz and Paul sat up late, making plans.

'So,' said Liz carefully, 'what you're suggesting is this. That I jet off to the Algarve and recuperate in the sunshine at this consultant's villa, in return for a little shopping and cooking when the great man himself is in residence — sort of caretake for him when the place is empty. But I don't have to clean or garden because there's a maid who lives nearby and sees to that side of things. Hmmm. It all sounds too good to be true. I suppose this surgeon . . . '

'Hugh Forsythe — he's a heart man.'

' . . . Mr Forsythe. I suppose he's not planning on bringing his family out, old Uncle Tom Cobleigh and all, so that the light cooking turns into a marathon slog in the kitchen? Which would be stretching my small talent to snapping point!'

'He isn't married, Liz. His wife was killed in that terrible plane crash last year. You remember, it had massive media coverage because it was such a disaster. Only a stewardess survived. Forsythe appeared to cope admirably on the surface, but it's generally felt he's taken on a work load that would break the back of a camel. The pressure must be incredible — but he's a man of furious energy.'

'One way of anaesthetising the pain of loss,' observed Liz quietly. She wished she hadn't made that jibe about old Uncle Tom Cobleigh and all. The poor man, he deserved everyone's sympathy.

'I have to say this,' ventured Paul, 'Hugh Forsythe is a very demanding man to work for. On occasions even junior surgeons find him terrifying in theatre. He came to the Hanoverian with a reputation for being a remarkable cardiac surgeon; but he will not tolerate incompetence at any price. He's not that much older than me — but he'll be offered a Chair before he's forty, mark my words.'

Liz's wide mouth quirked. In her limited experience the professorial type was hardly overflowing with personal warmth. Her mind's eye projected on to Hugh Forsythe: thin grey hair, already balding at the pate, watery eyes behind round steel-framed spectacles with thick distorting lenses. And bad-tempered to boot!

'You won't see much of him,' said Paul comfortingly. 'He uses the villa as a sleeping base while he works at this clinic he's helped to set up. Or he locks himself away in his study to write up his research. You should be able to cope easily — with a bit of help from Mum over the next three weeks.'

'I'm not worried about that. I'm not daft — and I can read a recipe. But I do wish Mum wasn't making this ridiculous proviso about us not saying I'm a trained nurse. She seems convinced I'll get roped in to help out at this clinic. And why not indeed? I can't envisage myself sitting about for a couple of months and doing nothing, can you?'

Paul grinned. Nurses had this tendency to feel they must always be on the go, and Liz was no exception. 'I feel awkward to be going out there on false pretences.'

'Why? Forsythe hasn't asked for a nurse, just whether anyone knows a student or someone free to help out for a bit. And I've no intention of telling

15

fibs *if* he should ask me direct. All the same,' Paul rubbed his chin with a thoughtful hand, 'the idea is for you to convalesce. I shall say you've had glandular fever, and may feel off colour on the odd occasion. H.F. will be sympathetic.'

Liz kept her doubts about that to herself.

'Just see he's fed and watered. And don't keep him waiting — if you can avoid it. And enjoy yourself, Liz — promise me that.'

A thrill of excitement was already teasing her spine. Liz sucked in her cheeks and hunched her shoulders. What an adventure! Apart from camping trips to France when Dad was alive, she hadn't been far abroad. Not on a plane. Paul was right: Portugal was going to be perfect.

★   ★   ★

Liz had always been perfectly content to go through life in the shadow of her clever, dynamic brother. She knew she herself was nothing special — just an ordinary sort of girl who loved and cared for people and wanted to do what she could to ease their suffering and be a useful member of society. Nursing she loved, and she really hadn't minded where she went to train. In her heart of hearts Liz suspected herself of being naturally unadventurous, of clinging to the safety of home. In Portugal she'd probably be homesick! But she felt sorry for poor Mr Forsythe — losing his wife so tragically when he himself was dedicated to saving others. With Mother's help she'd worked out some lovely meals to set before him; at least she could make sure that he had a nourishing diet and plenty of fresh fruit and vegetables, even if he was unlikely to enjoy much of that wonderful Portuguese sun.

One advantage of wearing uniform all day was that off-duty clothes could be kept to a minimum. Just one suitcase was all Liz was packing for the flight. She wasn't terribly interested in clothes, for she saw herself as small and dumpy, high fashion being for girls tall and elegant and much more poised. She just knew her face would look ridiculous 'done up' with blushers and complicated eye-shading and strongly tinted lipsticks. Her own colouring was soft and fair, her hair with its natural curl easy to manage.

At the airport she bought a copy of the *Nursing Times* to read once the two-hour flight was under way, tucking it into her hand luggage. Then it was time to wave goodbye to her mother and Auntie Meg and board the plane.

Committed. No backing out of it now.

Liz grew hot in the crowded cabin. She struggled out of her sweater, longing for a cool fruit drink. She hoped it was just the novelty of it all and not that wretched fever making her pulse throb so and her palms turn slippery with sweat.

To her left, the window seat was

already occupied by an elegant older woman in a pearl-grey linen coat, her white hair delicately rinsed with rose. Unlike the rest of the noisy cluttered holidaymakers, the lady travelled light, black crocodile handbag tucked down the side of the seat, a pile of glossy magazines settled in her lap.

Liz was trying hard not to stare, but wasn't that calm profile familiar? An ex-patient, perhaps, such a striking face would not quickly be forgotten.

The plane seemed full now. Take-off should be moments away if they were running to schedule.

Liz's attention was suddenly diverted by a flurry of activity at the front of the aircraft. A latecomer had entered just as the engines were beginning to thunder. The man was pausing to exchange words of greeting with the two air stewardesses, in their jaunty red hats and dresses. He looked to be a regular traveller on the Faro flight, and Liz could have sworn he was thanking them for holding the plane for him. What a cheek! Whoever was he? Chairman of the airline, or what?

Tucked beneath his arm was a silver-monogrammed black leather briefcase, and his midnight-blue suit with its discreet chalk-stripe spoke eloquently of Savile Row.

Liz felt compelled by unseen forces to view his progress down the aisle towards her, unsmiling now, with total disregard for the heads that lifted and the eyes that stared, the women admiring, their menfolk speculative. Only one woman ignored the stranger, and that was Liz's companion in her seat by the tiny window, attention fully absorbed in the society pictures of the *Tatler*.

The latecomer paused in the aisle, found the locker above his seat jammed with anoraks and carrier bags, so stowed his briefcase over Liz's row instead. She caught a fleeting impression of rangy height and lips compressed in annoyance — which only served to emphasise rather cruel good looks, slightly mitigated by the lock of thick dark hair which had dropped windswept across one impatient eyebrow.

He sat down and fastened his seat-belt without giving the matter a second's thought, then unfurled a copy of the *Guardian* in which he immersed his uncompromising head.

Liz shivered unaccountably and concentrated on the novelty of getting safely airborne. Behind her legs she had stuffed a straw bag crammed with odds and ends insisted on by her mother: barley sugar to suck during take-off, emergency food packages of bread and eggs and long-life milk. Spare tights! But not, it was clear, the nursing journal Liz wanted now to read. Which must be in that plastic carrier-bag (along with her folder of recipes) in the locker overhead.

Stewardesses were already moving down the lines of passengers offering drinks and snacks and duty-frees from their trolleys. The pallid young man on the right was snoring delicately. Liz felt sure she could squeeze past without disturbing him, he was so slightly built. Once in the aisle, by standing on tiptoe she could extend her lack of inches to delve deep into the locker interior and locate her plastic bag by feel . . .

As she stretched upwards the scarlet tee-shirt pulled out of her jeans, revealing an inordinate expanse of winter-white flesh which Liz preferred concealed. Her left hand came down to tug the shirt back into her waistband at the same moment as her searching right hand located the plastic bag and pulled it towards her. A black monogrammed briefcase slid over the edge and descended straight for the head of the sleeper below.

Liz had excellent reaction — the driving examiner had commented on that when she passed her driving test first time within weeks of her seventeenth birthday. It was just unfortunate that her fingers should have caught the zip-tag and slid the zip apart. 'Ouch!'

muttered Liz. But at least she'd grasped the briefcase before it brained the sleeping young man. There was nothing she could do, though, to prevent the mess of papers cascading everywhere.

The man in the midnight-blue suit was seething with ill-contained fury. 'Hell's teeth!' he fumed. 'What the devil are you up to?' He looked nasty enough to have sprung out of Hades itself.

'You can see it was an accident,' Liz flung back, stung to the quick. She nodded towards the young man, still sleeping, peacefully unaware of the drama taking place around him. 'He might have been hurt if that lot had landed on him!'

'If you weren't so careless it would never have happened in the first place. Look at my papers — I had them all in order!'

Liz pushed the random armful towards him. Someone added another lone sheet which had floated three seats down. I'm blowed if I'm going to apologise! vowed Liz crossly. Arrogant, ill-mannered so-and-so!

Bestowing on the enemy the most withering scowl she could muster, Liz found her *Nursing Times* and settled back in her seat for an uninterrupted read. To add to her chagrin her hands were shaking like some schoolgirl's. 'It wasn't your fault, dear,' murmured her elegant lady companion kindly, and Liz felt sillier than ever. Gradually the inner seething evaporated and the incident passed from her thoughts.

It was several minutes later that she began to be aware that her neighbour appeared to be having trouble with her breathing, her eyes fixed in mesmerised distaste on the double spread photographed in violent and horrific colour detail which Liz had been carefully studying. The nursing care of burns injuries.

'I am sorry — that was thoughtless of me,' she apologised. 'I'm a nurse, you see. I quite forgot that this sort of thing can be very upsetting to people who aren't used to it.' She stowed the journal out of sight beneath her seat, and offered to fetch the woman a glass of water.

This involved clambering out into the aisle and finding a stewardess who supplied ice-cubes, water and a glass. Liz's elbow accidentally rustled a corner of Mr Midnight's newspaper and they exchanged cool stares of dislike. But the woman drank thirstily and sighed with relief. 'That's better,' she apologised. 'Stupid of me to be so squeamish. Serves me right for being nosy!' Really, I'm perfectly all right now,' she insisted, guilty to see the concern reflected in the girl's anxious grey eyes.

'I'm so glad,' responded Liz warmly. 'But it was entirely my fault.' All the same she found herself wondering about that exquisite poreless maquillage which disguised the woman's true skintone. Would a sidelong glimpse of some admittedly grisly photographs be sufficient to turn a member of the general public dizzy with fright? Or might there be some underlying illness concealed by Estée Lauder and a clever hand?

Liz really couldn't decide; matters of life and death and grave injury all nurses learned to take in their stride. And it was an occupational hazard to find yourself making snap judgments on the state of the health of others. She folded her hands in her lap and passed the time observing her fellow travellers in their jovial anticipation of the holiday to come.

'Since I've deprived you of your reading matter, please share mine. If I may say so without giving offence, these pictures are much more fun.'

Liz smothered her rueful grin with a polite show of thanks, though the contents of *Harpers Bazaar* were not really her cup of tea. Her neighbour's eye had swept over Liz's jeans and well-washed tee-shirt as if to say young ladies would be better off studying fashion and beauty than poring over medical matters. Perhaps the figures on a nurse's monthly salary cheque would open this expensively dressed person's eyes to reality.

All the same, it was quite amusing to leaf through *Vogue* and discover that the latest model girls had been culled from the ranks of Oxbridge under-graduates. Liz relapsed into fantasy: and here is Elizabeth Larking from the Royal Hanoverian Hospital modelling evening gowns, along with Sue, a student nurse from Guy's, and Judy from the Royal Free who is a second-year on Women's Medical. That would be the day, dreamed Liz, closing her eyes and leaning her head back on the seat, visualising herself as lanky, svelte and authoritative . . . the type who would capture the admiration of Mr Midnight across the aisle instead of those undisguised and withering scowls.

'Would any of you care for something from the duty-free trolley?'

Liz shook her head, but the pallid young man sprang magically to life, stocking up with whisky and cigarettes as if his life depended on it.

Mrs Elegance, as Liz had christened her, bought perfume in a smart black and white package. Guerlain — French, the best. 'For you,' she insisted in her melodious voice. 'In reparation for being such a nuisance.'

It was so unnecessary that Liz was lost for words. She stuttered out that she couldn't possibly accept . . .

'Oh yes, you can. It gives me the greatest of pleasure to reward one of our nursing angels for her devotion to such a thankless and poorly rewarded profession.'

It sounded to Liz like a speech from a play. But the eyes held such warmth and generosity of spirit that to refuse now would be churlish and rude. 'I can't thank you enough,' she beamed, opening the package with genuine delight and exclaiming over the beautiful scent. 'Shalimar . . . mmm, it's quite delicious! I shall love wearing this. How can I possibly thank you?'

'My son always tells me I have more

money than sense, so don't thank me when for once I'm using it wisely. I don't imagine a nurse has much over to spend on luxuries, and I adore giving people surprises. 'I'm Anne Leigh Bycroft, by the way. Do tell me your name, dear.'

'Elizabeth Larking. Only mostly I'm called Liz.' Anne Leigh Bycroft — of course! The actress . . .

Across the way Mr Midnight was standing up to remove his jacket. Liz saw the way his nostrils flared as he picked up the sensuous perfume drifting from behind her well-scrubbed ears. Speculative eyes burned down upon her. How easy it was to read the man's contemptuous thoughts . . .

Little idiot, smothered in stuff only a woman twice her age could carry off!

Liz decided his back was almost as expressive as his nasty face. All the same, her eyes could not help but linger with a certain curiosity on the broad shoulders outlined by a clinging white cotton shirt — beautifully pressed by little Mrs Midnight sitting docilely at home while her husband jetted about the globe making money.

Anyway, why should Liz Larking care what the man made of her, a fleeting stranger passing by? Liz turned her attention back to Mrs Leigh Bycroft and fell into deep conversation which saw her through the rest of the flight.

# 2

'*Lamento, Senhorita*, no such a parcel has been handed in.'

'It wasn't exactly a parcel,' explained Liz anxiously. 'A plastic carrier containing a magazine, apples, a box of tissues — and my file of recipes. I left it over there,' she pointed to the chairs ranged along the wall near the baggage carousel, 'while I grabbed my case.' Not having two pairs of hands! she grieved to herself. And what use was a scruffy bag of oddments likely to prove to anyone else, for goodness' sake? Thank heaven Mr Forsythe wasn't arriving until the following weekend.

She turned away from the desk in confusion. Her first experience of flying, the routine of an airport quite unfamiliar — what was one to do? In her panic she would even have asked Mr Midnight for help, had not he and

Mrs Leigh Bycroft, unhampered by luggage, been seen with Liz's very own eyes strolling out to their waiting cars while she and all the other tourists had formed an impatient throng, all eyes on the tunnel disgorging at an infuriatingly slow rate their precious suitcases and holdalls.

At least nothing had gone wrong with the hired car. A brisk young man with dark skin and flashing eyes handed over the keys of a clean white Mini when Liz had produced the necessary docu-ments. The surgeon wasn't much of a cartographer, if the scrawl of his hand-drawn map was anything to go by. And the directions were hardly precise.

'Twenty minutes beyond Faro take the turning on your left marked Bull Ring.' Very amusing, when you were struggling to master left-hand drive for the first time in your life — and in darkness now, worried Liz, venturing on to the highway in a confusion of whirring windscreen wipers and undimmed headlamps . . .

Three-quarters of a tense hour later the Mini's head-lights picked out a low white building, its windows shuttered and silent against the night: the farm on the map, a roughly scribbled oblong in red Biro. And ten yards on, down a sandy track flanked by the dusty jigsaw leaves of fig trees, she should discover the Casa de la Paz.

Casa de la Paz. The House of Peace — what could be more welcome to a weary traveller? Liz found herself driving alongside a dense green hedge which must mark the boundary of the villa gardens. She wound down the window as she saw the gatepost, and there inscribed on blue-and-white tiles was what she was seeking, her home for the weeks to come, the Casa de la Paz.

Warm air flooded into the car, heady with the scent of orange blossom. Liz felt better already. It had tried to snow yesterday back home! At the end of a winding drive lay the spread of a large villa, its front door carved and studded and sturdy enough for a cathedral. In the lock was a heavy old key, and on the step terracotta urns filled with waxy richly-perfumed Madonna lilies. It was like a film set, and feeling herself but a humble extra, Liz opened the door and went in.

Luisa the maid must have known she was coming and left the lights on. Liz fetched her case and her remaining hand luggage — thank goodness she hadn't left everything to trust while she waited at the carousel — and called a nervous hello. But as she had expected, the villa was quite empty. Too weary now for major exploration, she dragged herself up the curving wooden staircase and into the first bedroom she came across. It had really taken it out of her, the journey and then this mystery tour in the black of night. Such fatigue brought home the debilitating effect of the glandular fever. And that wide bed with its white knobbly-cotton coverlet turned down in readiness for the sleeper was just too temptingly inviting.

Her case abandoned in the doorway,

the exhausted girl tumbled forward on to the bed — unwashed, unpacked, and fully dressed — and within the space of seconds was lost in the limbo of a heavy dreamless sleep.

★ ★ ★

Hugh Forsythe was tired too. He had gone direct from the operating theatres of the Hanoverian to catch his flight; and from Faro to the Clinic, dropping in on friends on the way back to the Casa, knowing that as usual the dependable Luisa would have every-thing prepared for his arrival. For once, he planned to take a week's break — really enjoy the sun and the swimming pool (it was still too early in the year to bathe in the Atlantic). Then when Paul Larking's sister arrived he'd get back to the grindstone and rely on her for his breakfast and evening meal. She'd been ill; but there was nothing like spring in Portugal for recharging the batteries. In the meantime he would eat out at the restaurants in Albufeira and enjoy some of that wonderful local fish, fresh from the morning's catch.

Yes, Miss Larking was welcome to the run of the villa when he was out all day at the Clinic. Hugh knew very little about her, but Larking was a decent chap and this unmarried elder sister of his was bound to be in the same competent responsible mould. Useful to have her there caretaking for the next couple of months. There'd been reports of gangs coming out from Lisbon to ransack the empty homes of the British. And though Hugh had given some thought to selling the place after Penelope's death, he had been too preoccupied with work to do much about it. Anyway, the place was a useful base for his visits to the Clinic.

He left the Renault in its usual spot by the farm, where Luisa would see it and know that Dr Hugh had arrived. Swinging his attaché case, Hugh came through the fig trees that backed on to the villa garden, ducked under a drunken old mimosa held up by a strategically angled wooden post, inhaled with unfailing pleasure the scent of citrus blossom — lemons and oranges and grapefruit bushes, every one planted by Penelope; and taking a bunch of keys from his jacket pocket, unlocked the back door and stepped into the kitchen passage.

★　★　★

There was a horrendous crash, a bellow of pain and outrage from the sprawling figure who had met up with Liz's suitcase in the dark.

The bedroom blazed with sudden light.

Drugged with sleep, Liz lay frozen, only her eyelids trembling as someone approached the bed and loomed threateningly over her. 'Hell's teeth!' snarled a voice that would make an Eskimo's hair curl. 'What the blazes are *you* doing here?'

Liz sat bolt upright, puzzled and

37

petrified at one and the same time. This strange room, and Mr Midnight! What on earth had happened? Was it a nightmare descent into hell — and he the Devil himself? But . . . the way the man was rubbing his elbow and grimacing roused her to automatic response.

'You've hurt yourself . . . let me see it. I'm a — '

Her words were cut off by an accusation that took her breath away.

'You're a trespasser, that's what you are. A squatter, I'll be bound. How dare you sneak into my house! Sleep on my bed!'

Liz's shocked eyes widened to the limit of their sockets. *His* bed? Mr Midnight-Blue's bed? She leapt off the white coverlet as if she'd been scorched. A paper fluttered to the polished wooden floor, and her antagonist (whom she now saw as equally astonished and indignant — and not actually out for blood) bent to retrieve the scrap. Hugh raked his head with a bemused hand and his hair stood up in feathery disarray. He looked almost human. Liz let her shoulders sag in a weary release of tension. Surely he must realise now?

'What the hell is going on here?' There was puzzlement in the deep voice, bewilderment replacing outrage. Hugh was staring at the map he himself had drawn in a hasty scrawl of red Biro.

'I'm awfully sorry, there seems to have been some misunderstanding. If you're Mr Forsythe . . . I wasn't expecting you till next week. I'm afraid I don't feel . . . '

Shock, weakness and an empty stomach caught up with Liz, and she dropped like a stone at Hugh's feet.

His bruised elbow throbbed angrily as he stared blank-eyed at this pathetic scrap of humanity collapsed before him in a dead faint. The young hooligan from the plane. And all he wanted was to get under a shower and into his bed. He shook his head in disbelief. Sorting this mess out must wait for the morning. The girl was trouble with a capital T. Hell let loose on that package flight he'd endured with this — this hyperactive *hippie* clambering back and forth and never sitting still for five minutes on end.

She was clearly exhausted; he couldn't kick her out at this hour of the night. But she was going to have to come up with a rational explanation for being in his bed, or he'd have a strong case for prosecution.

Hugh nudged the heap of girl with a toecap of black ice. She didn't move. Her head lolled like a doll's, strands of pale hair spilling across the curve of her cheek, the eyelids mauve above feathery lashes.

There was only one thing for it. Hugh knelt and gathered her into his arms.

Liz awoke next morning to find she had been most unceremoniously dumped in a downstairs bedroom at the far end of the villa, slung down like a bundle of old clothes on one of a pair of twin beds. In her crumpled red shirt and sticky jeans she must look such a scarecrow! But . . . as she recollected the night's events, indignation soon began to burn.

Hugh Forsythe must have thrown her down just like that, gracelessly, as if he'd brought her along to a jumble sale, abandoned her in the foulness of his mood. And what had he done with her things? Liz was all set to catch the next plane home.

Just look at that! An angry hand had wrenched those nice silky blue curtains with such aggression that the fabric had been dragged away from its wooden pole. But peering through the gap at Liz was an inviting cascade of pink bougainvillaea backed by a perfect azure-summer sky. And this was still early spring.

She ran confused fingers through the tumble of her fair hair. Who would have believed it possible? That grim-faced stranger on the plane turning out to be Hugh Forsythe, eminent cardiologist from the Royal Hanoverian in London. No thick-lensed specs, not a trace of a balding pate, shoulders very far from stooped. And no sense of humour either! To him, she was just some irresponsible little fool. Even worse, he'd taken her for a squatter! How could he have made such a mistake when he knew perfectly well Dr Larking's sister was coming out to the Casa? What on earth could have gone wrong?

Blinking dazed grey eyes, Liz looked about her. Actually, to be honest, this was a very nice and comfy room. And she specially admired the white-painted furniture, hand-decorated with delicate sprigs of spring flowers. She found herself getting excited about what lay beyond the locked french door of her room, leading out on to the beckoning garden.

But of course she wasn't going to stay. How could she, after . . .

Liz bit her lip, recalling how she'd thrown Hugh Forsythe's precious papers about, muddling up his research, jog-ging his elbow. Not to mention grimacing at him like a hooligan when he'd looked so sour about her wafting perfume. Small wonder he couldn't see any resemblance between Liz and brother Paul. Someone tall, dark and majestic with Paul's cool brand of competence — that was the paragon Mr Forsythe must have been expecting.

Well, she certainly couldn't have it out with him, not like this, looking like a scarecrow. For Paul's sake too, she couldn't throw in the towel so soon and run back home to Mother.

'Here goes,' decided Liz bravely. 'Plan of campaign. Battle tactics. Tidy yourself up, act contrite, throw yourself on his mercy. And play the invalid if it's likely to win any sympathy. But where the dickens has my stuff got to?'

The first door she opened revealed an en-suite bathroom, every last inch tiled in glowing apricot. The next door led out into a passage, and Liz all but went headlong just as Hugh Forsythe had done in the small hours. There lay the clutter of her packages, apparently thrown against the outside of her bedroom door with scant regard for her valuables. 'The eggs!' groaned Liz, searching her bag for a scrambled mess. But amazingly enough nothing had been damaged. Of course the recipes and their folder were irrevocably gone, but 'One trauma at a time,' she sighed resignedly. 'Let's take the trespassing charge first.'

Half an hour later Liz ventured forth, determinedly bathed, shampooed and looking her best in a very feminine dress of palest pink cotton. Her palms were clammy, but she wiped them on a tissue, opened the french doors of her room and stepped out on to a sunlit terrace spilling over with pink and purple bougainvillaea.

Now to beard the lion in his den — well, more of a sea-lion, judging by the scene that greeted her out there in the pool. For a moment Liz's attention was distracted by the sight of real lemons and real oranges growing on glossy-leaved bushes. She reached out wondering fingers and touched one of the fruits. It looked ripe! Could that be possible? And that frothy yellow mass was surely mimosa . . .

Already the sun was pleasantly hot. In the glittering waters of the turquoise pool a seal-dark head was storming up and down in a relentless driving crawl. Liz bit her lip uncertainly, then went to sit quietly in one of the cane chairs set out at the poolside.

'Come here!' barked the sea-lion.

Liz stiffened at being spoken to like that, and the curve of her mouth grew hard. Disdaining the steps leading out of the deep end, Hugh Forsythe was heaving his powerful body out of the water, shaking off the drops that clung to his skin, raking the wet black hair off his forehead. For a surgeon he was in surprisingly good shape, she found herself considering with reluctance. No stoop, no paunch, not a lax muscle or a spare pound of flesh. Once tanned he'd look downright . . .

Liz pulled herself together sharply. 'Mr Forsythe,' she began crisply and with an assurance that narrowed the thoughtful black eyes resting upon her. 'About last night, I — '

'Shut up!' snapped Hugh, towering over her now as he drew himself to his full height, way over the six foot mark. He was pushing the fingers of his right hand into the angle of his jaw, a brawny left arm raised so he could concentrate on the dial of his waterproof watch.

Liz had to tip her head right back just to see his face. She knew all right what he was doing; taking his carotid pulse, checking the wave of pressure which indicated the pumping action of his heart, the rate, the strength, the rhythm. He'd be particularly interested in the rate — something athletes did regularly to stress the cardiovascular system, spurring themselves on to greater fitness, pushing the rate higher every day they trained. A bruise was already darkening on the muscle above his left elbow. It looked sore. And the surgeon was returning her examination with an unsubtle scrutiny that was very hard to meet. Nevertheless Liz forced her hostile grey eyes to clash against his.

Watching for his reaction with a strange unease, she explained who she was: Elizabeth Larking, sister of Paul Larking, medical registrar at the Hanoverian.

'*Younger* sister!' stated Hugh in tones of disgust. For once he was prepared to concede that it was his own fault for jumping to conclusions. He hadn't asked for details — lack of time and lack of interest accounted for that. A spinster in early middle age was what he'd had in mind. A polite genteel lady who would keep herself to herself and an eye on his needs at one and the same time. And what had turned up instead? A dizzy blonde with an eye to the main chance. Far too pretty for her own good . . . or his.

'I'm going to need a chaperone,'

muttered Hugh as he frowned down at the top of Liz's shiny shampooed head. 'I think I'm in need of care and protection.'

'I beg your pardon?' Liz was still anxious to make a good second impression . . . though she couldn't help remembering that it was first impressions that counted. For Paul's sake. She couldn't let her brother down. And though initially she had been full of sympathy for Hugh in the tragic loss of his wife, it was difficult to sustain this in the face of his bullying rudeness. Such an insensitive man he was turning out to be — arrogant, dominating. He had all the fabled qualities of surgeons in novels, a man to whom the world owed homage.

'Paul Larking's little sister!' When he wasn't bellowing at you that voice was distinctly compelling, with a honeyed, hypnotic resonance. Definitely rather sexy, mused Liz, relaxing her guard for the first time since they had met and smiling at this sudden apparent friend-liness. No one was all bad; she'd never met anyone she really and truly disliked. The thing was to seek out Mr Forsythe's finer qualities.

'You could have fooled me.' His eyes assessed her, from the tip of her silky head to the white espadrilles on her small feet. 'No, you're nothing like your brother. Good job too.'

It was Liz's turn to look surprised — put that way it didn't sound very flattering.

'No,' Hugh continued, still keeping that thoughtful eye on the puzzled face upturned bravely to his. 'Clumsy, care-less, inconsiderate . . . I just couldn't see *you* in an O.R. theatre. You'd be a menace — mixing up the patients, trip-ping over the machinery, jogging the surgeon's arm. Tell me, have you always been so badly co-ordinated?'

Liz had taken as much as she was going to stand from this hateful man. There were times when actions could speak louder than words, and this was one of them. Without thinking, she shot an arm out and hit him square in the midriff. He teetered on the brink of the pool, lost his balance and plunged in backwards.

Her pink dress was spattered with dark splashes. For one heart-stopping moment delight inflamed her — a triumph immediately dispelled by recognition that she had acted with extreme foolishness. Had that been the shallow end the surgeon might have suffered an injury to more than just his pride. He certainly did not look like a man with any sense of humour . . . just as well she had not bothered to unpack . . .

Without waiting to find out, Liz turned hurriedly on her heel and was about to make a hasty getaway when, it seemed with the speed of the devil, Hugh Forsythe was out of the pool and beside her, fingers digging into the soft inner flesh of her arm and preventing any further hope of flight. Hell's teeth! cursed Liz with an inward gasp, but I've done it now. She was caught by the shoulders, turned against her will, forced to face her adversary.

'Let me go!' she grated between clenched teeth.

'Not so fast, my beauty. We have a few matters to sort out.' But he released her, planting himself decisively in her path, his body gleaming with crystalline drops of moisture.

Liz strove to act bold — though her legs beneath the pink skirts trembled. 'If you imagine I'm prepared to stay here to be insulted by you — ! I've been ill. If I have a relapse it will be your fault, *doctor*.' An ominous throb was drumming in her temples and raising a nerveless hand she could feel the blood pulsate beneath her fingertips. Lest her antagonist should take further advantage of her evident vulnerability, she added defiantly, 'And if you're hoping for an apology you're in for a disappointment!'

He actually smiled. 'If I wanted an

apology I should get one.' The assurance made Liz wince. It was only too easy to imagine Hugh Forsythe dealing with nurses and patients alike. Woe betide any who crossed his path or displeased him. 'However, since you fortuitously chose the deep end for your display of histrionics, there's no real harm done. Under the circumstances I'm prepared to be magnanimous.'

He strolled over to where he had left his towel, giving Liz the chance to make her getaway. But she stood rooted to the spot with indignation. He slung the towel about his neck, like a boxer, and came back to block her view of the gardens.

'What was the matter with you? A breakdown through stress, did your brother tell me? Your teaching job got you down? No, on second thoughts, it couldn't be that, you don't look much older than a Sixth-Former yourself. I must be confusing you with someone else.'

'Just as you confused the date of my

arrival,' Liz pointed out through tight lips.

The doctor shrugged as if it was of no importance after all. 'I'm a busy man. My head is full of weightier matters. I was expecting a middle-aged spinster suffering with her nerves, and what have I got? A schoolgirl with . . . what did you say?'

'Glandular fever. And I'm twenty-two — hardly a schoolgirl.' Here it comes, thought Liz resignedly, Paul got it all wrong, saying Hugh Forsythe wouldn't be interested in any personal details. Now he's going to quiz me about everything down to the state of my bank account.

'Nasty at your age — infectious mononucleosis.' Hugh rolled his tongue with relish around each syllable. 'The presence in the blood of a large number of mononuclear white cells, one of the characteristics of the disease.'

Blind the layman with science, scowled Liz, itching to let the doctor know she was less ignorant of the

53

medical facts than he assumed. But Mum had been so adamant. Liz had literally to keep her mouth shut tight.

'I take it they've done the Paul-Bunnell Test?'

'Of course.' To the best of her knowledge there were no other specific tests for glandular fever. Deliberately Liz stared past the doctor to where the grounds sloped down to acres of rough pasture on which a herd of goats grazed among wild vines and hazy blue flowers like tiny lupins. In the far distance she could discern a line where ocean met sky, and she judged there must be a beach within short walking distance beyond that clump of pines.

The surgeon waved a lordly hand encompassing the whole spectacle. 'You'll get a decent rest out here. I shan't bother you much over meals. Mostly I shall be working at the Clinic.'

Hooray for that, was Liz's secret reaction. Since I've lost all my precious recipes.

'Apart from this week — which I'm

taking as a breather.' He checked his stainless steel watch. 'I think I shall skip lunch today. You can fix me a late breakfast instead.'

If there was one thing her parents had inculcated into their children it was that manners maketh man. And orders must be prefixed with please. Mr Forsythe, Liz had already decided, was a very rude person. She herself was never rude if she could avoid it: it was her nature to be pleasant and constructive. But so help me, she vowed at that moment, if it's in self-defence Hugh Forsythe will get as good as he gives! Gaining my SRN has given me a new confidence. I may look as if I was born yesterday, but I've seen life and I've coped with death. And I've the confidence of a great profession behind me. 'Will scrambled eggs suffice, then?' she enquired sweetly, 'until I can get out to the shops.'

Hugh nodded, settling himself for a doze in the sunshine on one of the cane poolside loungers. 'Ask Luisa about the markets — she'll be here any minute.' He called Liz back as she turned to go, adding wearily, 'Luisa is a family friend. Please try not to upset *her*.'

Liz swallowed hard, swung on her heel, and went to investigate the kitchen. The sight of modern equipment and enchanting Portuguese crockery stacked neatly in the range of darkwood cupboards should have heartened the most reluctant cook. The floor was marble and the walls gleamed with their decorative blue-and-white tiles. Off the kitchen was a pantry with a second huge refrigerator and a freezer; if the place was under siege an entire battalion could brave it out there for months. Except that both fridge and freezer were empty.

The smaller fridge in the kitchen was more helpful, though. Luisa had bought in the basics, and they looked comfortingly familiar: bread rolls in a plastic bag, butter — perfectly recognisable as such though the wrapper said '*manteiga*'; and a rather scrawny yellowy chicken over which Liz cast a doubtful eye, recalling despondently the recipe for Chicken Chasseur which had disappeared along with the others. Was it an omen? she found herself wondering. Perhaps Mr Forsythe was going to turn her into the nervous wreck he had been expecting.

Breakfast should not prove too much of a hassle. But supper — oh dear!

When everything was ready, oranges picked from the garden and freshly squeezed, eggs cooking gingerly, rolls — for that was all the bread she could lay her hands on — toasting under the grill, and the long refectory dining table laid for one, Liz rang the handbell she discovered on an antique chest in the hall.

To her surprise Mr Forsythe appeared almost immediately. And he had taken the trouble to shower and change into white jeans (with a French label, Liz noticed) and an elderly and loose-fitting cotton tee-shirt, faded to a dusty black. Liz guessed he must keep a permanent wardrobe of clothes out at the villa, to save luggage when he travelled. The marble floors of the passage ways were cold underfoot, so he had slipped on a pair of battered leather mules for comfort. Hornrimmed glasses and a distant air of abstraction as he sat down with a pile of papers on the table by his plate, warned Liz he would not welcome any attempts at polite conversation, so she served him quickly and left him alone.

Having no one to talk to was going to be the worst thing, she was just thinking, standing by the sink with a cup of coffee raised to her lips, when a tapping at the kitchen's side door made her start.

'Luisa!' she greeted the maid thankfully. 'Do please come in — there's no need to knock. I'm Liz — and I'm so pleased to meet you. Do you speak much English?'

They regarded each other shyly and Luisa accepted the cup of coffee quickly offered. 'As long as people speak to me quite slowly I can understand,' she explained in her strongly accented voice. 'I come every day in the late morning when I shall not be disturbing to anyone here. I tidy the kitchen, I wash up — you should not have done so for me! — I make the beds and see to sheets and all washing. There is a machine, I will show you. And later I come back and water the garden — the Senhor Forsythe, he loves his garden, you know.'

'I'm sure he does — it's quite beautiful. I'm looking forward to exploring when I've been to the shops. You will tell me where to shop, Luisa? Where is the best place for meat and for vegetables? And I should be grateful to be shown over the house so I can get my bearings.'

'*Mas devagar, se faz favor!*' protested the woman, laying a gently restraining hand on Liz's shoulder. 'You speak too quickly, *senhorita.*'

As they set off to tour the house and grounds Liz soon discovered that her new companion moved about at a pace designed to conserve energy in the heat, slow and very erect as though she bore on her head an imaginary load; plump and dignified. Luisa had no children but lived with her married sister on the farm Liz had driven past in the night. Her skin was olive, mingling with the brown of her hair and eyes, and she dressed in shades of brown and black regardless of the weather or the sun beating down outside.

It was deliciously cool inside the house. On the ground floor was a vast L-shaped living area, the great fireplace piled with logs which Luisa lit early each evening and cleaned out next day. The dining room with its carved pine furniture and refectory table led off from the kitchen, this Liz already knew. But she was surprised to discover two more double bedrooms on the ground floor — each with its en-suite bathroom; apart from the two master suites on the upstairs floor. From a passage beyond the room in which she had slept came the sounds of typing.

'I must speak to Mr Forsythe about money for shopping,' she explained to Luisa, who could now get on with her own tasks.

Liz knocked sharply to make herself heard through the clatter and was told to come in.

'I thought I would get along to the shops now, Mr Forsythe. Perhaps you would care to give me the house-keeping a week at a time. That would probably be the easiest way.' She felt quite proud of her efforts over breakfast and waited hopefully for him to comment. But in vain.

'I'll have to go to the bank,' came the brusque reply. 'Take this for now.' He put a handful of notes on the table beside him for Liz to pick up. She felt strangely hurt by this, though she could not really explain why. It was the impersonality of the transaction, the implication that she was just a 'thing' with a job of work to do. Human contact was unimportant.

She tried again. 'Can I get anything

for you? Cigarettes? A paper?'

His lips clamped together with what looked very like annoyance. It made Liz feel uncomfortable, but she strove not to care.

'I'm not made of money,' he said impatiently, just like her father used to when she needed extra pocket money! 'English papers are a ridiculous price out here and I certainly don't have time to bother with them. As for cigarettes, I do not smoke and,' he gave Liz a very old-fashioned look, 'I should hope, young lady, neither do you.'

'It's not very popular among doctors these days, is it?' Liz commented ambiguously. She didn't smoke as a rule, but Hugh Forsythe was not going to be allowed to dictate to her whether or not she should.

He raised his eyes from studying her bare legs revealed by brief white shorts, smiled — yes, actually smiled — and leaned back in his chair, arms linked behind his head.

Now his hair had dried she could see

the threads of silver at his temples. But that grin, sardonic though it was, did wonders for the man. It changed his whole image from grumpy middle-age to what he really was — handsome, dynamic; and brilliant to have achieved so much by his mid-thirties.

Liz's pretty flushed face betrayed her thoughts so clearly, too young, too inexperienced to dissemble. It took Hugh by surprise to see the sudden dawn of liking and admiration mirrored in those clear grey eyes. He felt quite touched — not that he had been aware that her feelings towards him were so negative; not that he would even have cared. Naturally he expected others to be impressed by his status and achievements; women had always made it obvious they found him singularly fascinating.

Watching the smile fade and those black eyes turn cold and implacable, Liz braced her shoulders against an unexpected chill. Suddenly to have found this condescending man so attractive made her feel frighteningly vulnerable. Her chin lifted with determination. It should not happen again, so far as she could prevent it. She would do well to keep out of Mr Forsythe's way.

Pleading a convalescent's fatigue, she avoided drinks on the terrace that evening. The surgeon dined alone on salad and chicken, lumpy packet soup in which he discovered a piece of boiled cardboard which, to Liz's mortification, he left pointedly on the rim of the soup bowl. Next time she would remember to add cold water gradually so as not to get those nasty floating lumps of powder. Fortunately her mother had taught her the art of making good coffee and a decent vinaigrette. She cleared away the dishes, tidied up, then surreptitiously sneaked away her own chicken salad to eat in her bedroom.

'Chicken salad *again*?' exclaimed Hugh when the same menu turned up again next evening. 'We should be eating fish fresh from the sea. Get Luisa to take you to the fish market in Albufeira. The pork out here is good too. And what about a ratatouille? Peppers and aubergines, tomatoes, onions, etcetera — '

Seeing Liz's glum expression, he searched for something kind to say about the meal she had just slaved over. 'Well, you managed to keep any foreign bodies out of the soup tonight. It was an interesting flavour. Any idea what?'

'Fish, I think,' muttered Liz painfully. 'It's difficult when you can't translate the instructions.' How it went against the grain to know she must be considered so inept. If *only* she could have the opportunity to prove to Hugh Forsythe that there were areas beyond the kitchen in which she could truly excel. But her cooking was turning out to be a disaster, and it was on those grounds he was judging her.

I should never have taken the job on, she reproached herself with passion, quite unaware of his bold all-seeing stare. I may be ruining the health of one of our most important doctors. Her slim fingers twisted in an anguish of remorse as she stared unseeing at the debris on her own plate.

'Penelope always kept a recipe book somewhere,' Hugh interrupted kindly. 'It may be in the study, I'll have a look for you. And I know we have a dictionary. Let's have a look right away.'

Mistaking his considerate suggestion for concern for the inner man, Liz trailed dutifully after the tall broad figure heading energetically down the passage. He was a little easier to get along with than she had expected after that disastrous beginning.

But there again, you never could tell with so unpredictable a character as Hugh Forsythe.

Just as well, mused Liz, my own brother's a pretty high-powered doctor himself. These seemingly god-like creatures are just as human underneath as you or I. I shan't be easily reduced to a state of mute adoration — even if I am sharing paradise with the Devil!

# 3

'Right, young lady, I'm about to demonstrate the creation of the perfect *citron pressé*. First pluck your fruit fresh from the bush . . . '

With the meticulous care worthy of an expert in the techniques of coronary bypass, the surgeon dissected lemons into a tall glass jug, dripping water from the swimming pool over the kitchen floor that Luisa had mopped not half an hour earlier. Droplets of moisture clung patchily to his oiled skin, as he stood at the counter in his brief black bathing trunks, wet feet planted astride as no doubt he stood at the operating table. Trust a man not to realise someone could break a limb slipping on that bone-shattering marble! Liz left his side and reappeared brandishing the mop Luisa had left near the side door.

'Leave that alone, and don't fuss.

You're supposed to be watching my every move. See — you need the sharpest of knives, and not too much sugar, as even the layman knows by now — '

There was something very familiar about this scene, Liz grimaced to herself. Hanging with bated breath upon the words of some lordly consultant. Here she was, stuck in the kitchen when outside the sun blazed down from glorious blue skies. She yawned rather more obviously than was polite but covered up with a quick move of hand to mouth, envying the way Hugh Forsythe was tanning to a hue so much richer and browner than her own fair skin could take. All the same, she was a nice golden colour and her hair was already more than a shade lighter. It hung heavily over her eye, so she tucked the recalcitrant lock behind her right ear and pretended it was all just fascinating.

Once she gave a gasp of warning as the knife flashed through a slippery fruit and the surgeon seemed about to lose a thumb from one of those precious hands. 'Do take care!' she couldn't help herself saying, and, with an instinctive reflex action her hand clutched at the smooth warm skin of Hugh Forsythe's back.

'Good grief, you're a bundle of nerves!' he remarked testily, so that Liz felt about six inches high. As it was, the height and power of him dwarfed the girl, her head reaching no higher than his broad bare shoulder. 'No doubt you'd faint at the sight of blood,' he was saying conversationally, making not the smallest attempt to sound anything other than infuriatingly patronising.

'No doubt,' she agreed silkily, though privately her lip curled in self-derision. Go on, said the teasing imp in her brain, tell him the truth. He's just showing off now in his latest role of master chef. Bide your time till he slices through an artery, then save his life and earn his undying gratitude.

'Of course, compared to working on

a heart valve this is crude hackery.' Hugh grinned to see Liz blench as the fruit knife slashed past his fingertips.

She caught his sidelong glance and responded with wide and ingenuous grey eyes. 'Have you ever cut yourself, Dr Forsythe?'

'*Mister* Forsythe,' he corrected her cheerfully. 'You address physicians as Doctor, surgeons as Mister.' He seemed to have forgotten her brother was a doctor too.

Liz batted her eyelashes and said, 'But have you ever, Mr Forsythe? Cut yourself, I mean.' A bubble of laughter welled up in her throat and her eyes twinkled a warning that the keen-eyed Hugh Forsythe was not slow to miss. He hesitated thoughtfully and his eyes lingered on that teasingly curved mouth in a way that Liz began to find alarming. Who, she found herself wondering, was doing the teasing now?

'Cut myself in theatre? Not memorably — though occasionally some whippersnapper houseman might think he's cleverer than he really is and nick someone's glove. Fortunately,' the low voice was emphatic and the dark eyes held warning to anyone tempted to play games, 'fortunately I have lightning reactions.'

So have I, considered Liz, with an inward grin, recalling that falling briefcase. 'I'd give anything to see you operate.' Unfortunately this was said on the spur of the moment and most sincerely meant; but scarcely in character with her position as head cook and bottle-washer. As soon as the words were out she would have bitten them back; but it was too late, the gleam was now in Hugh Forsythe's eye. He snorted with laughter at the absurdity of such a wish, suspecting a naïve attempt to flatter his ego.

'My dear girl, you'd be out like a light at the first incision, getting under my feet as is your wont. Pass me that sieve, unless you want your toes trampled. And fetch me some ice-cubes — '

Don't you ever say please? fumed

Liz. Gosh, if I was his houseman I'd do more than nick his gloves for him. I'd stick the ice-cubes in his rubber boots, that's what!

'Now put that in the fridge for half an hour, then bring me a jug and a couple of glasses and you'll discover just how good this tastes.'

There was an outside staircase leading from the garden up to the arched balcony of the master suites. Halfway up these stairs was a flat sunbathing area which Liz had made her own for private sunbathing. Hugh did not seem to use the outside staircase, though she could sometimes hear him come out on to the balcony, and could smell the whiff of smoke from his occasional cigar as he leaned on the parapet and gazed down towards the sea.

She had put out a sunbed and left her paperback novel underneath in the shadow, with the straw hat for when things got too hot to be bearable. Her white bikini was on the brief side for wearing about the villa, so she usually covered up with a discarded striped shirt of her brother's. With the frayed sleeves rolled up over rounded brown arms and the collar painstakingly unpicked and discarded, Liz thought the final effect rather practical. That it emphasised her decidedly nice legs and tiny feet and looked more than just fetching, she had certainly not bothered to consider.

Unbuttoning the shirt, she stretched out, displaying herself to the sun. Her digital wristwatch was set to warn when the half-hour was up, and at its insistent buzz she struggled to her feet, wiping her hot face with a tissue and reaching for the enveloping shirt.

'Your lemon, sir!' she proclaimed with cheerful humour, setting jug and glasses on the low rattan table beside Mr Forsythe's chair.

'Thanks . . . ' came the vague reply, 'have some yourself.' The dark handsome head was bowed in concentration; secure, mused Liz dryly, in the knowledge that no call to wait on some woman or see to a meal would interrupt *his* precious time. It was a man's world all right; for a woman to succeed she must deal with all the mundane tasks and double her efforts if she wanted a career as well. It was certainly true you had to be twice as good as any man to make your mark. Liz peered enviously over Hugh's shoulder and discovered that the object of such fascination was a catalogue of surgical instruments. More of the same lay strewn at the surgeon's sandalled feet.

She attempted a diversion. 'Yet another glorious day. I feel as if I'm living in paradise!' She dropped into a nearby basket chair, sighed in ecstasy, and cupped her chin in her hands. The scent of mimosa hung heavy on the air, the fluffy, yellow bobbles just starting to bronze with the end of their flowering. The brightness and colour of every-thing was outstanding, and Liz gazed about her with relish, feeling she could never tire of such vivacity. How Mother would gasp at the sight of geraniums grown into great spreading bushes of red and pink and mauve, rampant cousins of the little pots she nursed so carefully throughout the winter on the kitchen windowsill.

Hugh had not even glanced up, sipping his lemonade as though it had been delivered by a robot, 'Hrmph!' his only comment on Liz's ecstasy. Matters of world-shattering importance occupied all his thoughts; that forthcoming paper to be presented at an international congress of specialists, the equipment needed to make everything up to date at the Clinic.

For a moment Liz considered seeking out Luisa for a chat — but decided she ought not to interfere with the maid's leisurely-paced schedule; there was work on the smallholding to be tackled as well as Luisa's duties for Senhor Forsythe. She was very shy, and clearly could not be persuaded that Liz too was a servant rather than a proper guest. And conversation was a matter of giggles and gestures, punctuated with the smattering of words Liz had managed to learn with Luisa's hesitantly smiling encouragement.

Suddenly a skinny grey cat stepped daintily out of a clump of mauve geraniums, her precise movements stirring the frilly leaves to release a scent like attar of roses. Liz exclaimed in surprise and stretched out a hand. Puss came running to her side on long thin legs, mewing plaintively for food. Liz tickled her ears and stroked the dusty grey fur, and the purring grew so loud that Hugh looked up, distracted from his work.

Liz smiled at him. 'No communication problems here. Oh, look, Miss Moggs appears to know her way indoors.'

'Then stop the dratted animal. The place will reek of cats.'

Seeing Hugh Forsythe's attention return to his papers Liz pulled a face. She got up and closed the french doors, her expression rueful. 'Sorry, Miss

Moggs,' she said in a Ned Larkin accent, 'but you 'eard what the master did say, you'm to stay out 'ere in the cold, cold snow.'

Hugh didn't move a muscle, his profile as imperturbable as ever. Humourless so-and-so! Heart man with no heart, grumbled Liz to herself, wondering if she dared sneak round the side and put out a few scraps by the kitchen door.

Sometimes she suspected her employer of being a mind-reader. He didn't even glance at Liz and the cat.

'I forbid you to feed that mangy creature. We shall never get rid of her if you do. And heaven knows why you think it's a she,' he added grumpily.

'Because of her sweet and friendly nature, I expect,' countered Liz with as much sarcasm as she dared. Hostile grey eyes tangled with those black ones examining her with blatant curiosity; held that bold stare until it was Hugh, losing interest, who turned back to the leaflet in his hand. The mangy grey cat had sauntered back to

77

its cool shrubby nook.

I just bet, mused Liz in her most private thoughts, Hugh was going to warn me off for daring to speak to him like that. I wonder why he changed his mind? . . . Oh, for someone to talk to, really talk to, hold an unthreatening conversation with, no hidden undercurrents, just a friendly chat.

She drained her glass, the sourness of the lemon making her grimace, her shoulders twitching in a little shudder. More sugar would be an improvement — that old sourpuss needed sweetening up a bit. She giggled at the thought, but covered her mouth with a tactful hand. Sourpuss! Quite apt, under the circumstances.

'Would you mind if I swim?' She stood up and looked coolly down at Hugh.

'Be my guest. I may join you in a while.'

She nodded, slipping off her shirt to reveal the white halter-top bikini. Hugh's left eyebrow soared to his hairline. A wolf whistle couldn't have been more vocal.

Turning her back to hide the ready colour staining her face and neck, Liz poised herself on the edge of the pool, toes curled and ready to dive. Since she had been ill the pounds had dropped off like magic, but in all the right places, to her own satisfaction. Even Liz had realised she was in pretty spectacular shape when she viewed her reflection in the full-length mirror. If anything she was showing too much of her assets ... she dived in a bit clumsily and hid herself away beneath the water, telling herself she was keeping out of the ultra-violet rays of the sun.

When eventually she clambered out again, those laser-eyes were waiting.' I hadn't realised just what that dreadful shapeless shirt was concealing.'

Liz gulped in exasperation. Here he goes again — everything the man says is a mixture of insult and compliment. Which do I deal with first?

'Thanks,' she said shortly. She picked up her shirt and was about to slip it over her shoulders when Hugh waved an arm in a gesture that stopped her.

'Please don't wear that thing, you look so nice without it.'

The 'please' was so disarming it took the wind right out of Liz's sails. She shrugged and plumped down in the chair she had been sitting in earlier. 'Aren't you going for another swim?' she asked brusquely, running her hands through her damp hair and ruffling it to loosen the clinging strands.

Hugh shook his head. 'I got immersed in these catalogues. We have the basic equipment organised, so now it's a question of deciding what else we can afford and what the likely workload would be. It's very tempting, all this new hi-tech equipment.'

Liz grinned knowingly. 'A gadget a day keeps the doctor in play,' she suggested naughtily, knowing full well she was treading on thin ice.

'Huh! I've no intention of succumbing to the lure of hi-tech medicine, just because some hospital down the road has got the latest thing in digital angiography. There's one helluva lot of equipment wasted or underused just because surgeons want the latest thing.'

He was actually addressing her as a rational thinking layman with a brain and opinions of her own! Liz wasn't going to waste the opportunity of some decent man-to-man talk. She leaned forward alertly, picked up a glossy brochure and bombarded her companion with the sort of questions she hoped an intelligent layman might put.

'Does hi-tech medicine mean the patient will get Rolls-Royce treatment?'

Hugh stroked his chin thoughtfully as he tilted his head, the better to permit his gaze to linger with approval. Larking's little sister was displaying an intelligence her fluffy blonde appearance somewhat belied. And this was a conversation he was actually enjoying.

Work, after all, was the subject closest to his heart.

The curiosity in the bright young face upturned to his, the lively way she listened and commented . . . 'Rolls Royce treatment — but at a price,' he explained. 'We have to justify such spending by demonstrating that it results in a considerable improvement in patient care. If not, then we stick with the tried and true methods.' He flicked dismissive fingers against the cover of a typically seductive and glossy pamphlet, then tossed it aside, looking seriously into Liz's interested grey eyes.

The contact became impossible to hold. 'I — I'd better fix your lunch,' babbled Liz hurriedly, reading in his expression something that disturbed her intensely — that for one moment the surgeon had discovered in her something worthy of his interest. Something that attracted him even more than the superficial appearance of her body in the flimsy white bikini.

Knowing her cheeks burned red in

embarrassment and confusion, she scrabbled on the ground by his feet, collecting together the heap of scattered catalogues and using the task to let her hair fall in a silken curtain and veil her glowing face. Her mortification deepened as she realised it was a replay of that scene on the plane. Only that time she had cared nothing for his approval, and now things were subtly changing between them. He had become physically aware of her, and she was emotionally enveloped by that undeniable charisma. No good could come of it, that was certain.

That afternoon Hugh broke his holiday to visit the Clinic. As he backed the Renault past her white Mini, Liz longed to say, '*Please* can't I come with you?'

But even as she plucked up courage at last to declare herself a trained and qualified nurse who would be specially interested to visit — or even help out if they were short-staffed — Hugh was gone in a spurt of exhaust and the Casa de la Paz was exclusively hers for the afternoon ahead.

Without its dynamic owner the place seemed to settle into a limbo of suspension. The very air was flat and stifling in the heat. There was a crackle of energy when Hugh was around, a lifelessness without him. Yet the anticipation of his return stirred a strange restlessness in Liz's mind, a nervousness even. She didn't know why . . . what she expected to happen that night. But there seemed every reason to fill the intervening hours with busyness.

If only Hugh had suggested taking her with him! moped Liz. Instead he went off with an eagerness that excluded her completely. Perhaps, she daydreamed with a rueful grin, he had staffed the Clinic with glamorous nurses far more entertaining than she. He must have some kind of a sex-life, mustn't he? Who could imagine a man of such compelling appearance leading a monastic existence for long . . .

'Elizabeth Larking, you could do

with a change of scene yourself. If you've nothing better to do than moon about wishing Mr Forsythe would make a pass at you, then you ought to be ashamed of yourself. Silly romantic little fool!'

Liz knew perfectly well that scolding conscience was right. She went off in search of Luisa to tell her she had decided to go down to the beach, and make arrangements for locking up the house. The Portuguese woman was pegging out the washing, her mouth full of clothes pegs. But she nodded and smiled over Liz's earnestly halting attempts to communicate by a mixture of signs and words. So charming, this Liz. So *bela*.

The scrawny grey cat was rubbing affectionately round Luisa's black-stockinged legs. It crossed to an empty saucer placed thoughtfully in the shade of the back door and mewed appealingly at its audience of two.

There was a rim of dried milk round the edge of the dish. 'Who's been spoiling you, then, Miss Moggs?' laughed Liz. It must have been Luisa, secretly disobeying her employer's testy instructions.

But Luisa looked surprised by Liz's expressive shrug of mystification. She tapped herself on the chest and said, 'No no. The *medico* . . . ees all heart.' She smiled fondly at the cat, imagining the doctor setting the saucer of milk carefully in the shade. It wouldn't be the first time he'd taken pity on the pathetically purring scrap. 'He ees all *heart*,' she repeated more confidently, winking hugely at Liz.

'You must be kidding!' exclaimed the girl, quite forgetting that communication between herself and Luisa was strictly of the pidgin variety.

As she crossed the meadow her thoughts of Hugh Forsythe were too intense for Liz to notice the thorns attacking her bare legs. What an enigma the man was; clever, ruthless, bad-tempered. Yet he could be moved by the piteous cries of a half-starved cat. Liz sighed deeply. She wished she could get Hugh Forsythe out of her mind. She wasn't sure that the discovery of his secret kindness to Miss Moggs made things any easier. She had a dread suspicion that this fascination he held for her now simply intensified the more she learned of the man.

'You've come out here to do a job. If he were anything other than a doctor, and you were anything other than what you are, Nurse Larking, would you take the slightest interest in what he says or does or looks like?'

'That's not fair!' Liz argued with herself aloud. There was no one around to hear.

'If you've got any sense — and nurses are supposed to have a super-abundance of the stuff — you'll keep out of his way and enjoy this rest-cure for what it is.'

'But I don't feel tired. I feel . . . '

'You feel what?' questioned the sarcastic voice of reason. 'Lovesick?'

'Oh, don't be silly! I was going to tell you I feel really well in myself. Just a bit

— a bit restless when Hugh's not around.'

'Oh, it's *Hugh*, is it now?' The voice was mocking. Liz flushed beneath her golden tan. If Mr Forsythe cared to invite her to join him at supper, she could scarcely refuse and plead tiredness *every* time. Besides, she was lonely, needed another human being's contact. And surgeon or not, Hugh Forsythe was a remarkably attractive man. On occasion he could actually turn out to be pleasant company.

Liz turned a corner and the cove was before her. An arc of soft white sand, hot beneath her toes, guarded by low orange cliffs like clumps of Edinburgh rock topped with a Persian carpet of spring flowers.

Only a handful of people sunbathed or strolled along at the water's edge. Liz spread her towel on the white sand and settled herself with a wriggle into its comfortable softness, carving out a hollow for her body to relax in. She closed her eyes and emptied her mind of thought, hands clasped behind her head as she worshipped the miraculous sun. How it calmed and soothed and cured all ills! If only you could bottle and market it, Essence of Sun. Then Hugh and she and all doctors and nurses would find themselves out of work!

It would never do to fall asleep in the sun. Liz sat up and probed her shoulders with cautious fingers. Yes, they were getting sore. Time for another dose of high-factor protection cream. Wasn't burned flesh supposed to smell like roast pork? Pork chops for supper that evening. And she'd bought olive oil and peppers and aubergines, and fat shiny tomatoes; and the most luscious strawberries, crimson and sweet, to be eaten with just a twist of lemon juice.

Wouldn't it be miraculous if Hugh ever suggested taking her out for a meal one night, giving her limited skills a break?

Liz propped herself on her elbows and watched three fishermen waiting for the perfect wave to launch their boat. None of the ripples seemed to take their fancy as they stood for ages with trousers rolled thigh-high in the shallows. Suddenly with a shout they heaved the boat forward and leapt jauntily aboard.

He might be back now, I really ought to go. Liz glanced at her watch and saw with a peculiar sense of impatience that the afternoon still stretched ahead. Why did time away from Hugh seem to pass so slowly? And even if he had come back, he'd be closeted in the study with his type-writer and his Bach tapes, humming tunelessly along with Glenn Gould, as the Canadian pianist crouched over those masterly Goldberg Variations. Or he might just allow himself to relax a moment and stretch out by the pool with the latest Jeffrey Archer.

Liz decided she'd had quite sufficient sunshine for one day. She'd go back and write some letters to the folks at home. Her head was throbbing a bit and she wished she'd brought some bottled water in her beach bag.

This time she chose the left-hand fork which offered a bit of shade from the overhanging trees edging the narrow lane. Along here the villas were smaller, less palatial, with interesting gardens that suggested these were not just holiday homes but permanent residences. When she imagined herself listening to the sound of her own name, floating clearly on the still air, Liz knew she had overdone the sunbathing.

But it came again. 'Miss Larking! Cooee! Miss Larking — '

Curiously Liz retraced her steps until she could see round the edge of a great shrub laden with flowers like fist-size white trumpets.

Peeping out from under the brim of a large sombrero was the actress Liz had met on the plane, Anne Leigh Bycroft, sheltering her exquisite complexion from the ravages of the sun. She leaned on a hoe as Liz crossed the narrow stretch of lawn, beaming that smile which had once captivated millions on the silver screen. 'In my day a suntan was frowned on. But you look disgustingly healthy, Liz — all those freckles on your nose. How's the glandular fever?'

'Vanquished, I think!' Liz crossed her fingers with a comical grimace. 'But you never can tell.'

Anne had already told her she was semi-retired; and had come out to her small villa to relax and learn her lines — in the summer she would be appearing at Chichester in an Ibsen play.

'You look as if you could do with a cool drink. Come in and chat to me for five minutes — I haven't spoken to a soul all day, apart from my son, on the telephone this morning.'

Liz followed the actress into her bungalow-style villa. 'Your son lives here on the Algarve?'

'Heavens! Didn't I tell you all about my beloved Richard? He manages a five-star hotel in the Monchique hills.

When I tire of my own company I stay there myself for several days. Of course the food is wonderful. Not that I'm a great eater myself.'

Liz privately considered the actress far too thin — but forbore from saying so. That kind of world, where looks and appearances were all-important, was not one with which a nurse would readily identify.

Anne was conducting a guided tour of the villa, flinging open wardrobes in both bedrooms to reveal enough clothes to stock a boutique; and all beautifully laundered and pressed.

'I'm not much into fashion,' admitted Liz, wondering if perhaps she was a bit peculiar. All this largesse — and she felt not a twinge of envy.

'Then you've never been in love,' stated Anne romantically. 'You wait till that happens! You'll want to rush out and buy heaps of new clothes so you look beautiful for your lover.'

Liz, in her baggy shirt and brief shorts, was embarrassed. She knew that her cheeks had flushed like a sixteen-year-old's. She'd never had a lover — and didn't see how she'd ever find time to fit one into her busy working life — rushing home to keep Mother company on her off-duty days, turning down party invitations because Mrs Larking worried alone at night in Orchard House. In the autumn, however, that would all change. Perhaps in London there would be lovers. And yes, she would discover the urge to dress to please men rather than simply for ease and comfort. Some of the doctors at the General had made it clear they'd have liked to get to know Nurse Larking a good deal better.

Anne Leigh Bycroft was pressing a white sundress on her. 'This should fit you. As you can see, I haven't worn it for a good many years — but I never throw anything away. You may like to take the hem up, but it's the sort of style that never dates.' She waved aside Liz's protests with an airy hand, leading the way back into her sitting-room, a cool oasis in the heat of the day.

Liz was beginning to feel a bit peculiar. Her limbs were heavy with a strange lethargy, and her temples throbbed. Surely it couldn't be that she was in for yet another bout of that confounded fever?

She struggled through a mammoth slice of Christmas cake and managed polite noises as the actress with such loving pride described each and every one of the numerous photographs of her husband, who had been a film producer of considerable reputation. The villa was crammed with memorabilia that had overflowed from Anne's Barbican flat. 'High time I got rid of some of my clutter. Richard won't want the bother of it all when I'm gone.'

Liz looked shocked. After all, the actress had the appearance of a woman in her late forties; even if she was sixty, it was not exactly old. Anne refused to reveal her exact age. She said the papers had been speculating about that for years, and she wasn't about to give away such a well-kept secret.

'You must get your employer to give you a night off from cooking. Tell him to take you to Richard's place — the Hotel Vicente. Richard will see you're wined and dined to perfection. I shall warn him to expect you. There's dancing at the hotel every night.'

'Oh, I should love that,' responded Liz with spontaneous pleasure. The idea of dancing in the arms of Hugh Forsythe was shivering to contemplate.

Anne seemed to be in a trance for a moment. 'Though I'm his mother, I must say my son is a very charming boy,' she said wistfully. 'How I long for him to marry and have grandchildren while there's still time for me to . . . But he doesn't meet *suitable* young women.'

Again Liz was disconcerted by a sense that the actress was anticipating her own death. Perhaps it was just a highly-developed sense of melodrama; perhaps it came from being too much alone. With the dress tucked at Anne's insistence into her bag, Liz said she must go and organise food for supper. But, if Anne was willing, she would very much enjoy popping over for a chat, since it was only a ten-minute stroll from the Casa de la Paz.

'It seems odd that you've never met Mr Forsythe, both of you living here in Santa Eulalia,' she commented.

Anne shrugged expressively. 'As you say, he's so busy. But I do remember his wife. She was frequently at the Casa de la Paz — a very striking woman, tall, with a mass of rich dark hair. Such a tragedy her death. She was a *Vogue* model, of course, wasn't she?'

'I really don't know,' said Liz slowly. But yes, that sounded the sort of woman Hugh Forsythe would choose to marry. As spectacular in her way as he was in his profession. No wonder the loss of Penelope had driven him into the refuge of his work! Medicine was his fortress, not a chink in its solid walls. He seemed to have slammed the portcullis on emotion. Where one might have expected to find bitterness over his wife's horrific death, there was instead this driving energy that was the hallmark of the man. A determination that where he had been helpless to save his wife, he would not waste a moment that could set others on the road to recovery.

Liz was finding even the ten-minute stroll a curious effort. Perhaps it was contemplating the surgeon's boundless energy that made her feel this weary. If only she could lie down here among the wild vines and the goats and the already-forming seedpods of the little blue lupins. Just a ten-minute nap and she'd be her old self once again. Damn this stupid glandular fever . . .

# 4

Head bowed and sun-streaked hair falling like curtains over her flushed cheeks, Liz scuffed a weary path across the meadow. When she reached the grounds of the Casa she sank down in the shade of a mimosa tree to rest for a few moments. She had no idea she was being watched.

From his vantage point, high up on the balcony outside his bedroom, Hugh Forsythe sipped from a glass of chilled white port and diagnosed too much sun. Silly girl, why wasn't she wearing a hat? Didn't she know an Algarve spring was like a decent British summer?

Hugh liked a woman to dress well, to make the most of herself. Liz just didn't seem interested. When he'd married Penny she had been modelling for Yves St Laurent . . . and that came after the Cordon Bleu course in London. They had been besotted with each other, right from the first. And four years later came the tragic disaster. Hugh drained his glass and sighed. He was over it now. Channelling all his energies into work had saved him from going mad. He'd even begun to enjoy his food again.

It was touching how concerned Miss Larking was over his meals, like an anxious dietician worrying over fibre and roughage and vitamin C. Fresh fruit and lots of salads. Hugh pulled a face — much the same as he'd eaten for lunch that day at the Clinic. It might be an idea to take her out for a meal. She wasn't the sort of girl to take advantage.

Hugh Forsythe MD, FRCS was tired of being yearned over; the meaningful eye-contact of heart sick scrub nurses across their surgical masks only made him more irascible. Coming out to the Clinic was therefore twice as refreshing, and his research project was going well. With Paul Larking's young sister he felt entirely comfortable. She didn't seem to realise she was a stunner. She certainly wasn't looking to make a conquest. Nice girl too; kind and gentle and concerned, even if her cooking wasn't going to set the world on fire.

By suppertime Liz was feeling pretty ill, weak as a kitten and with a pounding headache. Her throat felt sore and she knew that was a bad sign.

It got dark by seven, and the air cooled down dramatically. Luisa always lit the fire and left a stack of logs ready by the hearth.

Hugh called Liz in from the kitchen to join him for an aperitif before dinner. She didn't know why he insisted on their eating together, since he generally had his head in a book. Tonight the last thing she felt like was drinking alcohol. Protesting, though, was too great an effort.

He stood with his back to the blaze of the fire, legs planted astride, a black cashmere sweater worn with the sleeves pushed up over tanned and muscular forearms, a lock of soft black hair falling boyishly across the broad planes of his forehead. 'You've done something to your hair,' he said as he handed Liz a glass of white port. 'I rather like it — it shows more of your face.'

Liz touched her hair with nervous fingers and the glass trembled in her hand. 'I . . . er . . . I just cut a bit off at the sides. It was so hot and heavy.' With her nail scissors she'd created an airy side-fringe on each temple. It was more practical than the heavy wings of fair hair and Liz had liked the effect herself. But she was stunned that her employer should trouble to notice — or to comment. He must take in more than she had realised. It was his inconsequential manner that so confused and unnerved a girl. Her ready smile faltered and faded.

Hugh's mouth tightened. Clearly he had spoken with too much familiarity. He picked up his book and went over to his chair, waiting in silence for the meal to be served.

In the kitchen Liz poured her drink

down the sink and greedily swallowed three glassfuls of cold water. She peered into the oven, wincing at the sight of the food. This was likely to prove the worst offering to date: thanks to her blinding headache she'd misread the temperature when she set the oven and the meat looked about as appetising as a tiger's dinner.

In the dining-room Hugh's eyes remained on the open pages of his book. Neither spoke. The only sound came from their manfully-chewing jaws, struggling to masticate the pallid pork. Liz sat tense, waiting for the doctor to explode. He'd point out all the dangers with relish: the bacteria in badly cooked pork which would not have been destroyed by the too-low heat. She squared her shoulders in readiness for the diatribe, silently willing him to get it over and done with.

Hugh pushed his plate to one side, dabbed the corners of his mouth fastidiously with a napkin, decided on another bottle of Vinho Verde to compensate for his unsatisfied hunger. Liz followed his movements with a gloomy eye. However many glasses did he get through each night? And without apparent ill-effect. Not that one would care to vouch for the condition of his liver.

He was using a postcard of Albufeira as a bookmark; he slipped it now between the pages and closed the volume with an air of finality. Liz hung her head and clasped her clammy palms in her lap, waiting for the inevitable . . .

When the hand came down upon her bare arm she almost leapt from her chair in fright. But the doctor's fingers were reaching for her pulse, a cool palm testing her burning forehead. 'I thought so! You silly girl, you should have told me you were feeling ill. I could have eaten out instead of putting you to all this work when you ought to be in bed.'

'My throat's a bit sore,' admitted Liz, her eyes burning with a sudden rush of helpless tears at kindness from such an unexpected quarter. 'I suppose I could be going down with glandular fever again. Oh dear!'

A large white handkerchief appeared from nowhere and she felt the pressure of the doctor's hand on her shoulder. She blew her nose and dabbed her eyes while Hugh made reassuring noises. 'Cut along to bed and get a good night's rest. I'll see to the washing up — *and* you needn't worry about my breakfast. Tomorrow you can come with me to the Clinic and we'll find out what's the problem.'

Immediately Liz bit her lip: what a nuisance she was being! Hugh clearly supposed she was nervous at the prospect of more tests.

'Nothing to worry about.' His black eyes searched her unhappy face. 'I shall take your blood samples myself.'

He must have noticed the flicker of tension in the girl's cheek muscles, for Liz knew well enough that such eminent mortals as consultants wouldn't have done bloods for donkeys' years. Nurses tended to be far more proficient at such mundane tasks, and the prospect of Hugh stabbing away at her tender veins wasn't especially thrilling. 'Thank you very much,' she responded meekly, and was shocked to hear him laugh aloud.

'I can guess what you're thinking now, *Nurse* Larking, but I don't imagine I shall give you cause for complaint. We'll take a throat swab too while we're at it.'

While his 'patient' sat there stunned and speechless, twisting her fingers in the mansize square of white cotton on which she'd dared to blow her nose, Hugh poured himself another glass of Vinho Verde to fill the corners the pork hadn't reached. He raised it to Liz and laughed again, a rich goodhumoured sound that rang in her ears, his face transformed with triumph.

'Did . . . er . . . did my brother mention it after all? I mean, there was no intention to deceive you; it just seemed irrelevant considering the job description. And — well, Paul and

Mum insisted I'd been rather ill and a proper convalescence was important before I did any more nursing.'

'Fair enough. You suspected if *I* found out you'd get dragged off to work in the Clinic.'

Liz turned away from the irony in those narrowed dark eyes. 'Well, Mother knows what I'm like. Given the least bit of encouragement I would be, too! You wouldn't exactly have to twist my arm . . . in fact,' she added on a quick catch of breath before Hugh stayed her with a peremptory hand.

'Oh no, you don't, young lady! I wholeheartedly agree with your family, and I shall make no improper suggestions regarding your taking on any professional commitments.' He was amused at the way Liz's eager face fell into dismay. 'Come on now. I'm prescribing bed and an early night for us both. Let's get these tests done and see what's the score. Then if you're genuinely getting bored I *might* suggest you help me out on the odd occasion.

But only,' he added warningly, 'if this fever turns out to be a temporary relapse.'

As his knuckles rested gently against her heated cheek Liz had to bite her lip to suppress the gasp that rose within her. 'Could just be a touch of the sun,' he mused, recalling the girl traipsing back from the beach without any protection on her head. He opened the door for her and there was little she could do other than obey. And how nice it was to be given such masterful direction when feeling too weary even to face the washing up, let alone make any sort of decision. Liz knew now she had been wrong in dismissing Hugh Forsythe as lacking in sensitivity. He understood exactly how it was with her. He seemed to possess uncanny insight into her very soul.

But there was one thing still puzzling Liz. She halted in the doorway and stared up into the surgeon's lowered face. He was so tall he could clasp the lintel with an easy hand while supervising her progress towards bed.

'But how did you guess I was a nurse?'

'Elementary, my dear Watson.' The sardonic mouth curved in that lopsided smile that turned Liz's bones to butter. There was a second's pause while his eyes teased hers, one second in eternity . . . 'Why else,' Hugh murmured wryly, 'would a beautiful young girl be sitting there on a tourist flight with her nose stuck avidly in the *Nursing Times?* You couldn't be anything other than a nursing student.'

Liz frowned in indignation. 'I'm *not* a student! I've passed my Finals. I'm a fully qualified SRN.'

'Wonderful! Now be off with you. You can regale me with the saga of Liz Larking on our drive to Monchique in the morning.' With a totally unexpected gesture, Hugh bent his handsome head and his mouth brushed the soft skin of her cheek. 'Good night, then.'

Liz reeled drunkenly down the passage as if the water she had feverishly downed had at the touch of Hugh's lips turned instantly to wine. She knew she wouldn't be able to get a wink of sleep after *that*! So it was doubly astonishing to find her next conscious realisation Mr Forsythe's voice telling her it was nine in the morning; standing at her bedside with a steaming brew of coffee, his hair still damp from the swimming pool and clad in nothing more than a brief pair of white shorts that left little to the imagination of someone who had been dreaming about him all through the night.

Before Liz could speak, a thermometer was thrust between her parted lips, while the curtains were drawn and the daylight streamed in. 'Pity — cloudy day. Still, I hope you'll not object to a tour of the clinic, if I swear on oath that my motives are not in the least suspect. I shouldn't offer you work there if you went down on your bended knees and said you'd do it for love.'

He was teasing her and they both knew it. The thermometer clattered incomprehensibly against Liz's teeth. 'I'd whaggageggaguch!'

Hugh gave the line of mercury a cursory glance. 'Good. Temperature's normal — must have been too much sun after all. Still, we'll get the tests done just to be sure.'

Liz bit her lip at being such a nuisance to the busy doctor. 'Please don't go to all that trouble — you've enough to cope with as it is. Honestly, I do feel better this morning . . . '

He looked down into the appealing face with its tumbling halo of sun-streaked hair, intensely aware of the perfection of fresh golden skin emerging from between white cotton sheets. If he didn't make tracks the consequences of this encounter might lead to neither of them getting to the Clinic today . . .

'Be ready for ten,' he said tersely, and the bedroom door swung to behind him in a slam of irritation.

Liz sipped her coffee with a forlorn air, strangely hurt by this sudden withdrawal of the doctor's concern. While it had lasted, it had been nothing short of miraculous: Hugh, bringing her coffee, acting solicitous, friendly and kind. Mr Midnight was but a stranger from the past with his scornful eyes and whiplash tongue. Even so, it was safest to remember these were opposing facets of one very complicated man. Brilliant — yet caring. Awesome — yet, Liz caught her breath on the realisation, dangerously easy to fall in love with.

She dressed simply in a floral-print skirt from Laura Ashley and a sleeveless white blouse, its shallow neckline trimmed with delicate broderie anglaise. With her arms bare, it would allow the doctor plenty of flesh to attack in his search for a vein. Not that Liz was truthfully anxious on that score: stoical by nature, she had never been worried by the sight of blood, though it was true there were nurses (and even doctors) who had to struggle with their natures to overcome revulsion.

She brushed her hair till it fluffed in shining waves about a face tanned to the shade of honey; added a touch of dark blue mascara to her eyelashes; and left the rest well alone. When they arrived at the Clinic an hour later, she was to be glad she hadn't been tempted to gild the lily . . .

The lovely scenery of the drive inland registered little on that first visit to Hugh's Clinic as she poured out the story of her life for his receptive ears. Occasionally he would make some thoughtful comment; but if he was at all surprised to learn that in the autumn she would be coming to the Royal Hanoverian, he hid his reaction beneath his customary air of cool calculation.

'They couldn't guarantee me a place till mid-September,' Liz rattled on happily, 'but under the circumstances that turned out for the best. I was intending to take up a temporary staff job at my old hospital, but with the glandular fever it was enough of a struggle just to make it through finals.'

Hugh was pulling out to overtake a cycling party of youths in black Bermuda shorts, concentrating on avoiding the wobbly wheels of one young rider on a spindly racing machine. Momentarily Liz was struck by the profusion of white iris growing wild by the wayside, the orchards beyond carpeted with golden daisies and silken poppies. 'Of course, only certain hospitals offer these advanced courses for SRNs. I was particularly interested in Intensive Care when I was doing my training and I'd been unable to come to the Hanoverian till now.' She explained why, with cheerful candour.

'Hmm,' said Hugh, changing down a gear as the road began its winding trek up into the cooler hills. Liz told herself to shut up. Just because Hugh Forsythe had displayed a bit of human warmth and kindness, it didn't mean he wanted to listen to all that chatter. It was partly nervousness anyway; a discomfiture arising from the intimate proximity of the two of them alone together in a small and enclosed space. She could smell the lemony soap he used in the shower, mingled with the warmth of his skin; study the tautly-muscled solidity of his arms and wrists revealed by the crisp white short-sleeved shirts he wore to the Clinic. On the back seat of the car was tossed a grey linen jacket, partly covering the briefcase and a black medical bag Hugh must keep out there for convenience. He was a highly organised man, streamlining his life to the nth degree, unwilling to tolerate the smallest irritation which threatened his schedule. No wonder the power of him made her shiver!

What brought him so often to the Algarve? Paul hadn't seemed to know himself. Research, he had suggested vaguely with a grimace; must be pretty important too for Forsythe to drive himself on with that furious energy.

Liz plucked up courage to ask, and was agreeably surprised to find Hugh trusted her enough to speak freely. 'I instigated a research project into the effects of a diet rich in olive oil on cardiac disease. The paper I'm working on now will be presented in the late autumn at an international congress here in Lisbon. It's a comparative study of blood-lipid profiles; and I've managed to come up with some very interesting results from the material I've been collating.'

'And you've been studying patients at this clinic?'

Hugh nodded. 'And here we are!'

It was almost tangible, the surge of energy emanating from the surgeon as he slid to a smooth halt in the parking space marked out with H.F. in bold white letters. Liz clambered out and found herself in a quadrangle surrounded by white one-storey buildings. Hugh was already striding ahead, and she was obliged to break into a run to catch him before he disappeared from sight. Inside the Clinic, though, all was calm and reassurance. Once through the doors it was easy to imagine sick people relaxing with relief and gladly putting themselves into the care of the smiling staff who came to greet them.

All the same, it still came as a bit of a shock to Liz. There she'd been, imagining awful things about Hugh and a bevy of sultry glamour-girls in skimpy white uniforms, waiting on his every frown, and ready to jump into bed with him if he so much as glanced in their direction. And instead . . .

She reddened with guilt and hung back behind the doctor's broad protective shoulder. 'You never told me the nurses here were *nuns*!' Their uniforms were certainly white and sensibly cotton, but their hair was clipped out of sight under white veils and the Sisters wore white stockings and sturdy white lace-up shoes.

'You never asked,' returned Hugh blandly. 'These are Anglican nursing Sisters from a community in Norfolk. We've built them a small Community House and Chapel just behind the main buildings. Don't look so incredulous . . . surely you never supposed I was running a harem?' He opened the door to his own office and ushered her inside. 'Wait here while I find the Reverend Mother and tell her I've brought in a new patient. Shan't be five minutes.'

But he was. Liz grew tired of staring at the shelves of books and the desk piled with papers. She peeked out into the corridor and contemplated the gleaming expanse of pale floors and the immaculate white paintwork. On the wall opposite was a plain wooden crucifix. Nearby, a small table, with a blue-and-white pottery vase crammed with yellow and white daisies. Farther down the corridor two wheelchairs were lined up neatly against the window wall, ready for use. Liz sniffed the familiar smell of hospitals and felt very much at home. But wherever had Hugh got to? Had he forgotten her so quickly?

The footsteps had approached so noiselessly from the opposite direction that Liz was quite oblivious of the Reverend Mother's arrival. 'Ah — Miss

Larking. There you are, dear.'

Liz spun round to find herself eye to eye with a lady much her own height, comfortably plump beneath the folds of her white medical coat, a crucifix on a long piece of black cord jostling with the stethoscope clipped casually about her neck.

'I'm Mother Flora.' Warm hands enclasped Liz's own. 'Now, Hugh's been telling me about your glandular fever, you poor dear, and the tests he wants to do today. But as he's tied up for the moment, I propose you let me show you our Clinic. Since you're a nurse you'll be interested to see where Mr Forsythe does his splendid and valuable work, eh?' With easy informality she tucked an arm through Liz's, and with no appearance of haste led her down passages and in and out of rooms and offices and treatment areas, introducing Liz to a procession of nuns in nursing habits so similarly possessed of a cheery calm (unlike the solemn briskness of many of the hospital Sisters

Liz had worked under back home) that Liz wondered how one was ever distinguished from the other.

'You'll doubtless be surprised to learn that our finances allow us to have a theatre with facilities for coronary arteriography — entirely due to the eminent reputation of our beloved consultant cardiologist.'

Hugh! . . . this extraordinary woman was singing the praises of Mr Forsythe himself, as if he were the Archangel Gabriel made flesh and admitted to the ranks of the Royal College of Surgeons.

'We have five permanent beds here for the cardiac cases Hugh is keeping under review. If the surgery is beyond our capabilities . . . requiring highly specialist equipment and a big team of trained staff, then Hugh will operate back in London. But I'm sure you will be aware of the cutbacks which have affected the amount of surgery London hospitals can now undertake.' Liz was nodding vigorously, aware of how frustrating that must be to a surgeon of

Hugh Forsythe's calibre, having the skills to save lives but forbidden to use them to the utmost because the Royal Hanoverian's budget was tight. 'Then of course there is our cardiac research project, instigated by Hugh, and the paper he's preparing for publication.'

Liz was fascinated by Mother Flora. Reverend Mothers surely were supposed to look like the one who sang *Climb Every Mountain* in that Julie Andrews film. But this woman could be any child's picture of the perfect granny, a print frock under her doctor's coat, her grey hair cut practically short, yes, but far from the shaven head of mythology with its crisp natural wave. But appearances can be deceptive, and the keen eye and the brisk, kindly air of authority told another tale. Mother Flora, assessed Liz contemplatively, was nobody's fool. She clearly knew Mr Forsythe very well indeed, and her liking and respect for the man and the surgeon was boundless. Liz felt, suddenly, very warm and happy inside

— and so glad Hugh had brought her to this remarkable place.

With rapt attention she devoured all she was told, drank in everything she was shown, admired the small but immaculate operating theatre with its stainless steel walls and space-age precision, scrubbed and gleaming and ready for action. 'I'm the general dogsbody around here,' explained Mother Flora in bland understatement of her role as administrator and surgeon. 'On Tuesdays I operate with an anaesthetist who comes in from Faro. Dear little man, terrified of Hugh! The clever stuff, of course, we leave to H.F. — save it up, if we can, for his visits.'

'Isn't it rather unusual?' ventured Liz, unable to suppress her incredulity that a Sister of Mercy should be a fully trained and experienced surgeon. Her companion just chuckled and led the way back to her office for coffee. 'I mean, back home women surgeons are pretty thin on the ground.'

'That's as maybe. But I've spent more than twenty years out in Africa in the Mission hospitals. You name it, I've coped with it. And not in conditions like you see here, I can promise you! Then when they thought I was getting too old for that sort of thing, the Community recalled me and told me to get myself over here and help set this place up. After all, Liz, since the days of the early Christian church the religious orders have recognised a clear duty to comfort and relieve the sick.'

'Of course,' smiled Liz. 'I remember now. The first hospitals were founded by monks, and the first nurses were the 'little sisters' of Saint Francis. I did a project on the history of medicine way back in my days in Preliminary Training School.'

They had paused just beyond the patients' single-bedded rooms when Hugh emerged from the farthest doorway, closing it behind him with particular care and standing there, oblivious to the fact that he was being observed, his head bowed in a moment of profound contemplation.

For no good reason Liz felt her heart gripped with an aching chill. The hand that slammed other doors resting so gently on the handle, the arrogant dark head lowered and troubled. Was someone dying there within Room Ten? Beyond even the combined skills of the Clinic's medical staff?

Liz couldn't bear to see for a moment longer the despair she read in Hugh's slumped shoulders. She turned her head away and with a wretched eagerness followed Mother Flora to her office for coffee. When Hugh joined them he found Liz responding to questions that might have been calculated to focus her thoughts on herself and on her family rather than his problems. He greeted her with a slanting ironic smile and eyes that concealed the direction his own thoughts were taking . . .

Hugh poured himself a coffee and sat down facing Liz. He was trying to picture her in the Hanoverian nursing uniform; a frilly cap perched on her upswept hair and the prim, starched collar settled about her delicate throat, accentuating the long stem of her neck. As a mental image, it was decidedly attractive.

'The boss been giving you a guided tour?' he questioned, imagining the suntanned legs sheathed in sheer black stockings. 'She's a formidable lady, is our Flora. Iron fist in a velvet glove, I can vouch for it. I just do what I'm told round here.'

Selfconscious as never before, Liz tucked her legs under her chair. Why was he staring at her so, here, right in front of Reverend Mother's shrewd gaze?

'Oh, go on with you!' chided the nun in wonderfully familiar and unabashed tones. She even managed to wink at Liz, who relaxed a trifle and concentrated on drinking her coffee with a steadier hand.

A young girl knocked and peeped round the door. 'Reverend Mother,' she said urgently, 'you're wanted on the phone.'

'I'll take it in Sister Cecilia's office. Leave you two in peace for a moment.'

Surely, mused Liz, that girl was too young to be either a nun or a nurse. Why, she was only a teenager! Beautiful too. Even in a brief glimpse, that was quite apparent.

She waited for Hugh to drink another cup of coffee and glance through the letters that were waiting for his signature. 'I operated out here on a young Arab prince two years back,' he said. 'Since then my reputation seems to have spread like wildfire throughout the Arab world. The only problem when they come to the Clinic is where to house the bodyguards.' He grinned boyishly across at Liz. 'That's where Flora reveals her iron fist. She sorts 'em out and tells 'em what's what — and then charges them some horrendous fee which she insists is a private matter between her and her Maker.'

Liz's brow cleared and she nodded with a smile. 'So that's what Reverend Mother meant when she said *you* keep

126

this place going. She said it was your eminent reputation that provided all that specialised equipment.'

'And backdoor treatment *free* for the local people.' Hugh signed his last signature with a flourish. 'I ask no questions for fear the answers should make me wince. But all my patients, private or no, get the best I can offer them. And speaking of patients, Liz, your hour has now come.'

He led the way to a small treatment room and Liz was ordered to sit and make herself comfortable.

'I can't get over Mother Flora being a trained surgeon,' she mused aloud. 'It seems so strange, her being a nun too.'

'I don't see why.' Hugh was opening cupboards and assembling all the equipment he was going to need. 'Mission hospitals are frequently staffed with medically trained Sisters of Mercy. Flora's first-rate, highly experienced. I've a great admiration for the dear old thing.'

'When you're in London, is she the

only doctor here?'

'No. We've a part-time medical officer from Lisbon, but he divides his time between us and another clinic in the north. You'll meet him — if you come here again, that is. Open up.'

Forestalling any reply, Hugh bent over Liz and shone his pencil torch into her mouth. He took up a throat swab and touched the sides of her mouth, then put the swab into a container. 'Looks okay to me,' he opined, depressing her tongue again with the spatula, while his left hand, resting on her hair, tilted her head back for a closer look into her straining throat.

He wrote on the label. 'We don't normally do bacteriology tests here. I shall have to send this off to Faro, and it will take about three days for the results to come back. The blood test will be quicker.'

He drew up the blood sample with a casual competence that made Liz smile a secret smile as she recalled how he'd read her thoughts. Like everything this man did, his technique was perfect. You couldn't fault him. She'd scarcely felt a thing. 'It's very kind of you to go to so much trouble,' she said again. 'I hope it's not wasting your time.'

He drew himself up to his full height, and regarded her with an air of scorn. 'You do like to go on, don't you,' he accused irritably. 'I suppose if the tests come back negative — as I damn well hope they will — you'll be wringing your hands and apologising about *that* too! Now get your skirt off and hop up on to that table.'

Liz went hot and cold from hurt and humiliation. Good manners certainly didn't count for much with a man like this!

Hugh regarded those flaming cheeks with raised eyebrows. What was so dreadful about taking your skirt off when you habitually spent most of each day wearing little more than two scraps of handkerchief?

'What's the problem? Forgotten your knickers?'

Liz's eyes were wild and wide. 'Of course I haven't! But wha — I mean, why do I . . . '

Two hands dropped on to her shoulders and propelled her towards the treatment bed. 'I should like to palpate your liver and spleen, if I may,' he explained with heavy courtesy. 'If it will make you feel more comfortable I can ask one of the Sisters to step in and keep us company.'

For answer Liz tugged at the elasticated waistband and let her skirt pool around her ankles, conscious that Hugh was not even going to pretend to look the other way. He was grinning broadly, and it roused in her the most negative of emotions. She'd gladly have stuck him with a blunt syringe if it could have wiped that bland expression off his face. The power and the glory must have gone to his head for all time!

Don't be such an idiot, hissed a little voice of sanity as she submitted tensely to the cool hands probing her liver and spleen. 'I'm looking,' explained Hugh seriously, 'for a sub-clinical hepatitis. And praise the saints, I'm not having any success.' His eyes were very dark beneath a mobile brow scarred with concentration, his lips compressed and firm. A lock of hair fell boyishly over the maturity of his strong face, and to her shame Liz wanted to push it back out of his vision. She closed her eyes and waited for him to finish.

'All the same,' he was saying slowly, half to himself, half aloud, 'I do think we'll check the liver function tests, to be on the safe side. I think we owe it to your brother Paul, don't you, to be especially thorough, since but for his thoughtfulness I should not be enjoying the services of so conscientious a housekeeper.'

Suspecting she was being mocked yet again, Liz held her breath and submitted to hauling up her blouse to allow his hands free rein. She felt pretty silly, though, lying there in her knickers while Hugh checked over the secret organs of her sweating body. 'Relax,' he murmured at one point, keeping a careful eye on her set face for signs of pain. 'That hurt at all?'

'No!' snapped Liz, dragging down her blouse and with a bad grace allowing herself to be helped down with a gallant hand.

'Good girl,' said Hugh in his kindly, clinical manner. 'Now I'm going to take you back home for some more pre-scribed rest.'

# 5

A white envelope with Hugh's name on, and a long blue flimsy airmail, were waiting for them on an antique chest in the hallway of the Casa. It had been a quiet drive home: Liz had pretended to doze most of the way — though she could hardly have been more wide awake. Adrenalin still surged through her and she was gently trembling with tension.

There he sat beside her, so close she could have touched him with the least movement of hand or arm. Every time he coughed or cleared his throat, or on one occasion muttered an oath as, swooping up to the brow of a low rise, he met a peasant cart meandering down the middle of the road towards them. The sound of his breathing, even — every nerve in her body was aware of him.

'Another billet-doux from the boy-friend,' observed Hugh with an amused glance at Liz's wild-rose cheeks. 'And what have I got here . . . aha, the *encantadora* Rosita!' He was scanning several lines of a flowing artistic script.

Liz said nothing. She'd told him before there wasn't any boy-friend, and all she'd got in return was another of those amused, speculative glances roaming over her, head to foot. Oh yes, it seemed to say; expect me to believe *that*!

'This is from some local friends of ours . . . of mine,' Hugh corrected himself with a quiet dignity that told Liz he was thinking of his dead wife, Penelope; a wash of sudden pity sluiced away any remnants of the sulks. 'They live over near Loulé. Would it put you out a great deal if I were to dine there tonight?'

In her usual well-schooled polite manner Liz assured her employer it would not — though the chicken in the larder wouldn't keep another day.

'And you're obviously still very tired. Another early night will do you good.'

And a break from you will do me good too — you're more potent than any virus.

Liz picked up her letter and went out into the garden. She settled herself by the pool and glanced up at the lowering skies. Rain wasn't far off.

It was from Pam, her brother's wife.

'Dear Liz, I'm playing secretary as your big brother's on call tonight. He's left me strict instructions to say it's all very well you writing home and telling us you're A1 and champing at the bit. You're to *take things easy* while you've got the rare opportunity. And we all endorse that, so you can quit feeling guilty, Nurse Larking. Doctor's orders.

'Don't forget Hugh Forsythe is expected back here at the end of next week, when a series of big heart ops has been scheduled for his mighty scalpel . . .'

Liz read that bit twice, biting her lip. No, Hugh hadn't mentioned it yet.

Well, there'd be some respite from playing chef for a few days, and *that* prospect wasn't without its compensations.

'Wish I could come out and grab a bit of the sunshine you describe so temptingly in your lovely long letters. I can just picture the Casa de la Paz, and Luisa, and the fish market in Albufeira. And since you're my sister-in-law I'm trying to keep my imagination *off* the topic of Hugh Forsythe in shorts. Yes, we all know he's a fitness fanatic. All the rest of the surgeons here have saggy middles!

'As you say, he's not a man one can easily feel sorry for. He's got so much going for him. Brilliant surgeon, the sort of looks that have all us physios and nurses yearning just to be noticed by the wretch. All that explosive energy — like a time bomb about to go off. Wonder what he's bottling up . . . ?

'Paul says give his regards to H.F. and tell him the Hanoverian's grinding to a halt without him. Don't you worry so about your mum. We popped over for a night last week and she and your Auntie Meg are having a whale of a time. They'd just got back from a weekend break in Norwich and were planning a trip together to York. Sorry, love, you're not missed.

'A big hug for your little self, Lizzie, from the two of us.'

Liz pulled out a tissue and blew her nose punishingly hard to stop herself from crying. Hugs and kisses didn't much come her way these days. All of a sudden she was overwhelmed with homesickness and a longing for a familiar face. Life was taking her in such strange directions now, with a rapidity that was frightening. And she herself was changing, her eyes on new horizons, her emotions in confusion. At least with Hugh away she'd have a chance to try and sort herself out in the peaceful quiet of the Casa.

★　★　★

Liz yawned and glanced at her watch. The glowing log fire was making her sleepy and she could no longer concentrate on the book sliding off her lap.

Hugh would be surprised to find her still up. He'd told her a little about his friends, Rodrigo and Rosita Vedras. In spite of her name, Rosita was a Londoner. She and Penny (Hugh mentioned his wife's name quite easily this time) had become friends when the Forsythes first bought the Casa de la Paz through Rodrigo's agency. He supervised any decoration or maintenance, and organised the occasional letting. Liz could just picture the couple: homely, friendly sort of bodies, welcoming foreigners settling into the Algarve and showing them the ropes.

Liz had found a jar of cocoa in the kitchen and mixed some ready in a mug to be warmed up when Hugh came in. He'd be glad of it, for the nights were surprisingly cold. They would discuss his evening out. He would be relaxed and amiable at the conclusion of another busy day.

She got up and helped herself to another glass of his favourite white port, then curled up once more, listening to the crackle of the burning logs. It was nearly midnight; she would wait up one more half-hour.

She must have fallen asleep.

Laughter and voices echoed in the hall. Lights snapped on. Hugh came striding into the sitting-room, followed by two other people.

Illuminated in the childish gesture of rubbing knuckles into blurred and sleepy eyes, Liz struggled to her feet, awkwardly tightening the belt of her robe.

'Darling,' a redheaded woman was drawling, 'you should stay with us. It must be so lonely here — all on your own.'

She caught sight of Liz. Emerald eyes snapped and a rich-girl's mane of red-gilt hair whipped across her shoulders as she swung back to question

Hugh. '*Não percebo!*' she hissed.

The parquet flooring was cold against Liz's bare toes. She bit her lip, wishing herself tucked up in her bed as Hugh had clearly expected. He hadn't bothered to mention her presence. A *servant* at this hour should not be found in the living quarters. He'd brought his friends back for a nightcap, and Liz herself was the intruder.

She felt hurt. Then, as she interpreted the Senhora's curious stare, on her guard. Curiosity and — could it really be anger?

Why should that be? Unless in the slight and dishevelled figure of Liz Larking, Rosita Vedras saw something to be jealous of. And glancing from her own brief white towelling robe to the glamorous Rosita's jewel-coloured silken shift, the exquisitely decorated face — coral-glossed mouth in full pout, almond eyes exaggerated with bronze-gold shadows — Liz was quite at a loss to guess why.

'You have a visitor, Hugh!' Rosita's

surprise was registered in tones that suggested Liz might have been discovered while Hugh was out beachcombing, a peculiar piece of flotsam washed up on the tide and rescued out of pity. The woman's coldly glittering eyes, however, told quite a different tale. 'A *visitor*, darling. You really should have warned us . . . '

Her fingers brushed Hugh's as she took the tumbler of whisky from his outstretched hand. He bent low and whispered something unfathomable in the exquisite ear. Rosita tossed her head and laughed so infuriatingly that Liz wondered how her husband could watch the two of them with such smiling equanimity. She gathered up her book and made to leave the room without any apology for being there. Who would have believed it of Hugh Forsythe? The idol had feet of clay.

Rodrigo forestalled her. He moved to her side, picked up her empty glass and handed it to Hugh for a refill. His perceptive eyes lingered on the bare legs and feet, the tumbled mass of fair hair, the charming face, flushed with the warmth from the fire — and indignation. The air was full of misconceptions.

'Thanks, but I really don't want another drink,' Liz insisted in a voice meant to demonstrate dignity and poise before a sophisticated audience. Somehow it came out wrong; small and timid and a trifle huffy.

This slight, offended *senhorita* with the piquant face and tremulous mouth was in need of care and protection. Against his wife's cutting tongue and the scowling eyes of their host! Senhor Vedras drew Liz down beside him on to the sofa. 'You must not rush away like this,' he murmured softly, taking her stiff hand in his, gazing into charming grey eyes wide with hurt and guarded tension. 'It is *we* who intrude upon your privacy. So tell me, *minha senhorita,* what is your name?'

Rodrigo's attentiveness towards Liz

seemed to exasperate the surgeon, who gave an exclamation of impatience. 'This is Elizabeth Larking,' he said abruptly, coming over to stand between the sofa and the fire, his cream linen jacket unbuttoned to reveal the crisp frill of his dress shirt. Aggressively he thrust both hands deep into the pockets of elegant black trousers, strong legs set astride as though in challenge over Liz, who sat transfixed by this magnificent apparition in evening dress.

The sight of Hugh had brought a lump to her throat. She waited for him to rescue her, her knight in shining armour.

Hugh was abrupt and to the point. 'Liz is working here doing some cooking for me. She's recovering from a bout of glandular fever.'

Thank you very much, Mr Forsythe! I'll get back below stairs this very minute. Pardon me for intruding . . .

But a little red devil was dancing in Liz's fertile brain. She absolutely refused to be intimidated by Hugh

Forsythe, or made to appear small before his guests. Liz Larking was no servant but a fully qualified member of the nursing profession — and proud of it!

'That is correct,' she acknowledged formally. 'You see, I'm a servant rather than a guest and should not in truth be hogging my employer's fireside. I will say good night, then, sir, if you will permit me. I am indeed more than a little tired.' The look of astonishment on Hugh's face as the quaint Victorian phrases tripped off Liz's naughty tongue was priceless!

The corners of her mouth twitched as she saw a questioning look register on Rosita's face. As if the sum of two and two might not be adding up to a straightforward answer after all. Why did people have these compulsions to jump to suspicious conclusions, smelling smoke where there wasn't any fire to speak of?

Hugh had raised an idiosyncratic eyebrow and was obviously striving to keep his features strictly in neutral. You troublesome young woman, said that articulate eyebrow, what are you up to now? One of these days you'll go too far. Such pert temerity in front of my friends! Just you wait until morning . . .

And forgetting she'd been afraid she was falling in love, Liz felt more than a trifle scared of the man himself as she lifted a defiant chin to complete her act.

'Good night, then, everyone. And good night to you, sir.' In spite of everything Liz was discovering a breathless, heady excitement in challenging Hugh Forsythe. Few dared; it was a situation he was unused to; her head was on the block!

She could all but hear the teeth grinding in fury.

But, 'Good *night*, Larking,' came the cold, unemotional reply.

★  ★  ★

Hugh was already thrashing up and down the swimming pool when Liz

145

crept out to pick the breakfast lemons.

Keeping well out of view, she peered cautiously through the glossy leaves of a lemon bush. What was the worst she could expect? An operation without anaesthesia? Even *that* sounded more bearable than the prospect of a tongue-lashing from Mr Midnight at his most irascible.

Stomach! Behave yourself and stop that churning.

Liz squinted accusingly down at her own taut contours. Talk about long-suppressed feminine wiles! She'd bought a bikini from a smart boutique in Praia da Oura, the like of which she wouldn't have dared be seen *dead* in but a few weeks back. *Scarlet*! With saucy white polka dots, and little bows on the side of the minuscule pants. And a strapless top you could only paddle in — if you bothered to wear it at all.

After all those salads she knew she wasn't exactly an eyesore; and they both had marvellous tans. As for Mr

Forsythe (and it seemed appropriate today to revert to thinking of the surgeon in the most formal terms), Liz was crossing her fingers he'd be so relieved to see her decked out in something other than her old stripey shirt, he'd forget her behaviour and cool his annoyance.

Even so, she wasn't going out of her way to confront him.

Tiptoeing back and forth with the breakfast things so Hugh could eat on the terrace in the early sun, Liz checked the table to make sure nothing was forgotten. Fruit juice, coffee, butter and toast. And Luisa's own marmalade from the garden oranges. Two lightly poached eggs would take no more than a moment.

Liz went back to the kitchen and set a pan of hot water on the gas to bubble.

'What the hell was all that about last night?'

Hugh had come up behind her so silently she dropped a plate with a clatter on the worktop. She caught it

147

neatly before it spun off the edge and shattered on the terracotta tiles. 'Whoops!'

Two strong damp hands gripped her bare shoulders and swung her about to face him, pressing the cold steel of the sink into her unprotected spine. As suddenly those hands let her go, curling into angry fists resting on his hipbones as Hugh glowered over her. Liz went pale beneath her tan.

'Making a fool of me in front of my friends!' he growled accusingly, scouring his wet hair with a fierce hand. No woman should look that enticing so early in the day. Liz was definitely asking for trouble. She must know the effect she was beginning to have on him — why else had she started dressing so provocatively?

'Some friends,' said Liz bitterly. 'Some friends, if they suspect you of having an affair with me.'

'That's ridiculous.' Hugh was staring across the top of her head and out of the window. Damn. He hadn't been wrong. And he knew well enough what Rosita was angling for. She was beautiful but stupid, wouldn't know the meaning of the word *subtle*. Surely by now she'd got the message that he didn't want her style of consolation.

'Well, of course it's ridiculous,' muttered Liz, biting an embarrassed lip. The red bikini wasn't going to justify its price at this rate. More of a red rag to a bull, the scarlet reflected like blood in the pupils of Hugh's glaring eyes. 'But I don't see why *I* should be ranted at. Mrs Vedras is the one with the nasty mind — jumping to conclusions!'

'If I want to fill my house with women I have a perfect right to do so!'

'I was only trying to help!' exclaimed Liz, more offended than ever. The last thing she had envisaged was embroiling herself in an argument over her employer's sexual activities. Of course he'd every right to bring Rosita here behind Rodrigo's back, if he so chose. But she'd make jolly sure she cleared out herself and got well away. 'I wanted to convince your friends I was . . . well, not what they were thinking. I wasn't deliberately wanting to annoy you.' It was a small lie, but what the hell. Hugh responded with a bark of incredulous laughter.

'Well, I admit I did exaggerate the forelock tugging when I saw you getting cross with me. No, wait! Let me finish. What I said *did* make Mrs Vedras think twice. I guess she's used to servants and thinks it only right and proper to be servile and obsequious. But you and I are used to the hospital world, and we know people just don't grovel like that any more.'

Hugh exhaled a gusty sigh as if weary of the whole matter. But he still blocked Liz's path, and the breakfast was out there getting ruined by the sun. Her darting eyes fell on Miss Moggs' clean saucer, left out on the window-sill by Luisa, and Liz recalled Hugh's secret kindness to the pathetic, hungry scrap. She shook her head and spoke her thoughts injudiciously aloud. 'I just don't understand you. Such a fuss about a little bit of play-acting, on the spur of the moment!'

'Fine,' snapped Hugh. 'Well, young lady, the second act is mine.' And with that he jerked her slight body against his and his brutal mouth descended upon her in a kiss that forced her head back until her neck felt it must surely snap. Almost fainting from shock and emotion — and finding herself as roughly thrust away from him — Liz reeled back against the scrubbed pine table.

Perhaps the man *was* mad . . .

'You beast!' she gasped, pressing the back of her hand against her bruised mouth. Her eyes were wide with shock, the pupils so enlarged they reduced the iris to a colourless rim.

Hugh leaned back against the dresser, arms folded, perfectly calm, observing with an almost clinical detachment the tachycardia accompanied by other symptoms of violent arousal. He had complete command of his own anger and used it as a formidable weapon to get what he wanted. He could switch it off at will.

His clinical observation was on automatic pilot. The girl might succeed in fooling herself, but he knew the truth. Like all the others, she was falling in love with him. And he read the same symptoms in himself. This was something he couldn't control. It was ironic to think of it. He would have considered himself too worldly, too experienced to be so vulnerable.

Anyway, she was far too young, and his life was too full to include her. He'd done what he intended — put her strictly back into line. The victory clearly was his — even if he'd acted like a chauvinist and beaten her by sheer brute strength.

Liz flinched as Hugh's parting words lasered into her brain. She repeated each one, committing that challenge to memory.

'That was my act in our little

scenario. The next move is yours, Nurse Larking.'

★　★　★

I'm going on strike. I shan't cook another meal until that arrogant beast apologises!

Pigs might fly. Oceans might freeze. Men like Hugh Forsythe can do no wrong. Act sensible, Liz. Don't flatter yourself he'd planned that kiss. It just happened — a result of proximity and mutual attraction.

Mutual attraction! She shivered violently as an icy finger teased the channel of her spine. She scowled back at that other self in the looking-glass, attacking her scalp with vicious sweeps of the bristle hairbrush. Hugh Forsythe was nothing more than a chauvinistic cross-patch. She wasn't in the least attracted to him — not any more. Did he think she was going to be bowled over by the fact that he was one of the VIPs of the surgical world? Well, he'd forgotten one thing about Liz Larking. Her brother was a doctor too, and he'd pulled her hair and she'd kicked his shins in years past. Hugh was no godlike figure to her, any more than Paul was. If ever she should fall in love it would be with the man himself, not the glamour of his profession. That was for storybook romances.

So why are your hands still trembling? probed that sarcastic little voice that refused to let her off the hook. That's right, put your hairbrush down and check.

'Steady as a rock!' muttered Liz doubtfully. 'Well, I'll show him I don't care. I shan't sulk in my room. If the next scene is mine to orchestrate, then I know just what I'm going to do.'

There was nothing in the fridge for supper — apart from half a dozen rolls in a plastic bag, a couple of eggs and a pint of milk. All part of my plan, Liz reminded herself grimly. There's no point in shopping today — not with what *I've* got in mind. I shall help Luisa in the garden instead. I've discovered a new and fascinating hobby since I've been here: gardening.

At five she went in to shower and change.

Just before six the Renault could be heard crunching up the gravel drive. And Liz just happened to be posing there on the turn of the stairway — he only had to turn his head to see her — when Hugh strode in like an electric storm, slung his linen jacket and black medical bag on to the hall table, and yelled, 'Liz!' his voice ricocheting off walls and ceiling and reverberating throughout the Casa de la Paz.

There she stood in the white dress Anne had given her, doused in that fabulous *Shalimar* perfume, her hair knotted up into an Edwardian bun and pretty as a picture. And Hugh didn't even glance her way but strode on and down the passage to his study. Liz stood uncertainly in the doorway and watched him gathering up papers on his desk and pushing them into his black briefcase with the silver initials H.F. emblazoned on to the leather. 'I'm here,' she said questioningly.

Hugh spoke rapidly. 'I've had an urgent call from the transplant team. I'm on the next flight home. It's a double job — heart and lungs — on a young man. Take me to the airport and bring my car back here.'

In the ordinary way Liz would have bridled at this peremptory command, but the urgency of this mission was undeniable and the nurse in her was well aware there wasn't a moment to waste.

'Right,' she said. 'Give me the keys and I'll turn your car round and have the engine running.'

'Good girl!' Hugh looked up for the first time and did a double-take. 'Hey, you weren't going out, were you?'

With a swift shake of her head Liz took the keys from his outstretched hand. Within two minutes Hugh was Mr Midnight once more, hurling himself into the passenger seat and cursing as she fiddled among the unaccustomed switches for the headlights. Night was coming on fast. She covered the distance in record time.

Hugh was out of the car and heading for the departure lounge almost before she'd braked in front of the entrance to Faro Airport. She watched him go, Mr Midnight in his business suit, formidable, all-powerful and distant as ever. She'd wanted to say *good luck!* . . . as if he needed luck on top of those outstanding surgical skills. Sadly she rested her head on the coolness of the steering wheel, feeling drained and weary. The second act had gone wrong after all. The intimate meal à deux in some wisteria-wreathed café was never going to happen.

What was it Anne Leigh Bycroft had said? Liz had been embarrassed by the actress's perception: but it was perfectly true. She'd never been in love. She hadn't ever wanted to dress to please a lover. There'd been no lover in whose eyes she had wanted to see the reflection of her own desires. Not until tonight.

She had been reckless in her daydreams . . . and at last she had reached the stage where, spurred on and driven by the jealousy brilliantly evident in the emerald eyes of Rosita Vedras, she had determined to make Hugh aware of her, too, as a seductive and feminine creature. Whatever the consequences . . .

And now he was gone — and he hadn't even said when he'd be back.

A tear trickled down Liz's cheek and plopped on to her lap. She sat there in Hugh's car, in his driving seat, her fingers resting on the wheel at ten to two where so often his own hands had lain, striving to summon up the energy to get herself back to the Casa de la Paz. Bereft of his presence.

When, terrifyingly, the door beside her was wrenched open on a rush of cold air, she cried out in genuine fear. But it was Hugh — his fingers closing over the flesh of her arm, urging her out into the chill dusk.

Feeling her tremble, he gathered an arm about her bare shoulders to protect her from the night. He was breathing harshly as if he'd run back to find her. 'The tests . . . I forgot to tell you . . . The results are back and everything's clear.'

Liz couldn't think straight. The tests. They seemed to be important . . . oh yes, that glandular fever. So remote now . . .

'Your throat swab had grown a haemolytic streptococcus which proves a mild tonsillitis. Liver function and blood tests absolutely clear.

'Must go now, Liz.' He gave her a big, brotherly, reassuring hug and sniffed the air. 'That perfume's far too powerful for a girl like you — Rosita's sort of smell. Gives me a headache!'

With her cheek pressed against the smooth cloth of Hugh's Mr Midnight suit, Liz clung there in a state of suspended disbelief. This couldn't be happening. It was all a dream. She didn't even mind about the perfume. Shy fingers traced the edge of Hugh's lapel. It didn't matter if he went away now. She'd be living off her memories for days ... If he should kiss her goodbye then her cup of happiness would brim over. Nothing needed putting into words ... not yet.

Adorable Liz — how can I bear to go away like this and leave you? ... man, don't be a fool! You've got your freedom to do as you please, why spoil everything just because this slip of a girl is gazing up at you with her heart in her eyes? Hugh bit back the dangerous inclination to throw sense and reason to the winds. Since Penny had died he had intensified his professional life to the exclusion of all else. Back in London he'd get things into perspective once more — a momentary aberration under a foreign moon.

For a second his fingers increased their pressure on her slender ribcage, then he was walking away from her, his voice carrying back on a note of irony. 'Don't burn the place down while I'm away . . . God knows when I'll be back.'

And he was gone.

# 6

Hugh parked the Renault in the space marked H.F. and strode into the Clinic. His tan had faded to a sallow tint and his features were harsh with fatigue. Mother Flora, as on every Tuesday, would be down in theatre with the general surgical cases. He bypassed her office and went straight to Room Ten.

He stayed there almost half an hour; the ritual of sitting and watching and going over it yet again in his mind. That still form in the hospital bed surrounded by the apparatus which kept her alive. Evidently over the fortnight there had been no change. That was, he supposed, something to be thankful for; change could only be for the worse, and her condition hadn't altered in many long months.

At last with a profound sigh Hugh got up and crossed to the window, his fingers massaging the tension in his forehead and cheekbones. No problems left behind in London; nothing his registrars couldn't cope with anyway. As usual it had been a packed schedule with little sleep . . . so much for a four-month sabbatical to see the research project to conclusion.

He'd taken a taxi home to the Casa — funny he should be thinking of the place now as home! — but she wasn't there and nor was her car.

Hugh went to his office and checked the in-tray for vital messages or letters, then the cardiac review patients claimed his attention. He unhooked his medical coat from behind the door and headed through the Clinic corridors. As he passed Room Ten again, the young pre-nursing student Mary was just going in carrying a mouth-tray, with a clean towel over her arm. At the sight of the surgeon her face lit up in a beaming smile and her huge dark eyes glowed a welcome. 'You're back, Mr Forsythe! It's good to see you.' Proudly she drew his attention to the tray in her hands. 'Liz showed me how to lay this up — gallipots for the fluids, cotton-wool swabs, artery forceps and . . . er . . . '

'Dissecting forceps,' prompted the doctor, his tired eyes crinkling with a smile of encouragement, concealing with his customary aplomb any trace of the surprise he was feeling at the mention of Liz's name. What on earth was she doing here at the Clinic? Or had he, in his fatigue, got hold of the wrong end of the stick?

It was a frown of perplexity, but Mary, a sensitive girl and most anxious to please, misunderstood. 'I'm going to do the mouth care now, Mr Forsythe. I'm sorry you found Room Ten empty, but I was only five minutes getting the tray ready, and when I came back I could see you there through the window. Sister Cecilia's always most insistent this patient must not be left on her own. Your orders, she told me so.'

Hugh laid a reassuring hand on the teenager's arm. 'Of course, Mary, of course,' he murmured soothingly. 'I'm going to keep my eye on you when you come to London to train in September. Any problems, you bring them straight to me — okay, lass?'

It was a relief to see the pride and the pleasure in those dark almond-shaped eyes. 'Where is Miss Larking, by the way?'

Mary hadn't a free hand, but she bobbed her head in the direction of the conservatory. 'In there with Kev, the Aussie, trying to make him behave himself. No one seems to know what's the matter with him. I think it's to do with him fainting several times and putting the wind up himself. Reverend Mother told him he must stay here till you got back, but Kev says he feels *much* better now with some decent meals inside him, and he wants to be on his way.'

With a conspiratorial giggle, Mary leaned towards the tall doctor, adding sotto voce, 'Sister's hidden all his clothes and Kev's hopping mad! And his smokes too. You should hear him swear! And he's made some — some very improper suggestions to me and Liz. She really tore him off a strip. Why, it even terrified *me*!'

Hugh opened the door to Room Ten and hurried Mary inside. Since she had been brought up in the Norfolk convent since her parents died, it wasn't surprising this exquisite child was naïve as a kitten. Nursing would either kill or cure, but he'd certainly have to keep a weather eye out for the ingenuous student nurse. Uncouth young medical students would do more than suggest improprieties. They'd be fascinated: a dark-eyed madonna with a vocation for the religious life *and* the profession of angels . . .

Pausing at the entrance to the conservatory, Hugh blessed the cover of a large palm. On more than one occasion he'd groused to Mother Flora about the difficulty of locating his patients among all this tropical green- ery the nuns were so enthusiastic about;

but, on the rare occasion, it had its uses.

Kev's strident Aussie tones could be picked up with no effort at all. He had clearly driven the other ambulant patients back to their rooms.

'Aw, now look here, Nursie, if you don't give me back my shorts I'll walk outta this nunnery in my 'jamas!'

Liz sounded terribly unsympathetic. 'Do that. You'll be a sight more respectable than when you turned up here. When your things have been washed and patched up, you'll get them back, so quit fretting.' There was a pause. 'Hold your arm out, please.' Then, 'Any more of that, Kev, and I shall forget I'm supposed to be a caring person! Now hold that arm steady.'

With stealthy care Hugh moved a frond aside. He could see Liz — looking ravishing in a white dress that accentuated her tiny waist and flowering hips, and a little white cap perched on her swept-up hair . . . where had the Sisters found that piece of frippery?

— bending over her patient. The only visible part of Kev was the back of his short-clipped sunbleached head. The sight of Liz was doing strange things to the rhythm of Hugh's heart. Like a guilty schoolboy he let go the palm and concentrated on the sound of her voice — and other sounds which indicated Kev's blood pressure was being taken.

'Whatcha writin' on the charts?'

'Information that will help Mr Forsythe make his diagnosis. He's one of the best heart men going.'

At that precise moment the heart man diagnosed that he might be going into fibrillation. He clutched at his chest to keep the organ under control.

'Aw, hell, what do I need with a heart man?'

'If there's something the matter with your heart, then H.F. will know it. All you have to do is wait here, have a lovely rest and lots of nice food, till H.F. gets back from London.' Liz's tone was wry, as if dealing with a hyperactive infant.

'If the guy's so bloody infallible then I guess this spider's web must be the Vatican Palace. Ouch, Nursie, that hurt!'

'Get away with you! We must have a blood sample for the tests. Put this cotton wool on the puncture and bend your arm up.' Liz raised her eyes to heaven, but smothered a grin. Kev was a bit of a handful and his language turned the air blue. He'd been back-packing round Europe and all of a sudden started fainting like some anaemic adolescent. Kev was big and strong and fearless — or he'd always believed so. And beneath his protests Liz could sense he was more than a little scared to find his symptoms had the Clinic staff puzzled.

'I haven't got any money, you know,' he blurted suddenly. 'I can't pay.'

Liz was stacking the equipment she had been using on to a trolley. She didn't make a big thing of it, but in passing gave Kevin's hand a comforting squeeze. 'No need to worry about that *here*. All we're after is the pleasure of your company.'

Kev had the grace to come up with a sheepish sort of smile. 'Sorry about the language. Nursie. I'll try an' watch it when the ladies are around.'

Liz laughed out loud. 'What's up, then? Aren't I one of the *lydies*, Mr Wilding?' It was at this point Hugh stepped out of the jungle of palms and was gratified to witness Nurse Larking turn pale beneath her tan and then a becoming shade of wild-rose-pink.

'Why, Mr Forsythe . . . ' It came out so breathless Kev gave Liz a very funny look. She took a firm grip on herself. This Aussie backpacker spoke as he thought. If he latched on to any vibrations between her and Hugh, he certainly wouldn't have the delicacy to mince his words. It would be all over the shop in no time.

Amazed by her own apparent self-control, she explained Kevin's case history to the consultant.

''Ts nuthin' now. I jes' wanna get on

my way, man. Guess I fainted from an empty tucker bag.' But he trotted back to his room, meek as a lamb, a hefty square-shouldered blond young man, brown as a berry and, Liz considered privately, looking ten times healthier than the doctor who was examining him with such clinical thoroughness. Hugh looked worn out, and her heart ached to see it. When he'd had a decent rest — that would be her chance to put to him the problem of Anne.

They drove in separate cars back to the Casa. Hugh was reserving judgment on the young Australian until he'd seen an ECG done the next day.

Liz was worrying all the way home because she knew there wouldn't be much to eat in the larder. A good hot meal was what the surgeon needed to revitalise the inner man. But Hugh poured himself a whisky, waved a dismissive hand and insisted he'd eaten on the Faro flight and wanted nothing else. Doubtfully Liz regarded the haggard lines of his sallow face; trust

171

Hugh Forsythe to have crammed in the most punishing schedule at a risk to his own health! It brought a lump of wretchedness to her throat to see this dull-eyed monosyllabic shadow of the man in the midnight-blue suit.

His voice too was slurred with fatigue. 'The last place I expected to find *you!*' As he slumped in a cane armchair, dangling a whisky tumbler from loose fingers, his glazed eyes travelled over the girl he hadn't seen for two long weeks. 'I'd like to know who decided you were fit for work, Nurse Larking.'

The last thing Liz was seeking was an argument, not with Hugh in this state of exhaustion. 'You told me my tests were clear. A message came from Mother Flora: the review file was on your desk here and she needed it urgently. I drove to the clinic where I discovered three of the Sisters were down with 'flu, and they were desperately short in theatre. I volunteered to scrub — had a wonderfully happy day.

I've been going back alternate mornings and helping out wherever I'm needed.'

A morose grunt was Hugh Forsythe's reply. 'I've had no ill effects whatsoever. On the contrary — ' Liz checked herself. She'd been about to blurt out that working made the days pass more speedily till Hugh's return. 'I've done the tourist bit too,' she added with determined brightness. 'Cape St Vincent all to myself, shopped at Loulé market, climbed over the Crusader castle at Silves. The weather's been simply glorious!'

The doctor's head was drooping on to his chest, his fingers loosening their grip on the emptied glass.

Liz knelt by his side, rescuing the crystal tumbler, lifting the limp hand between hers. It was so cold! She rubbed it between her own two warm palms, felt the skin roughened from scrubbing for those endless operations Hugh had completed back in London. 'Bed for you now, Mr Forsythe,' she whispered as if to a child, drawing him to his feet and guiding his blind steps towards and up the stairs.

In the morning; that was when she would speak to him about Anne. Something had happened while he'd been away.

★ ★ ★

Liz had been down in Albufeira, shopping for fish at the morning fish market, and bread at the bakery on the corner which sold mouthwatering cakes and pastries. She'd stood there a good five minutes, casually dressed in white shorts and faded red clinging tee-shirt, her hair tied back in a red spotted handkerchief, dusty toes thrust into white espadrilles, mulling over a delectable display of little marzipan fancies: ships and fish and prawns and other novelties. Finally she chose a boat for Luisa and a shrimp for Anne — a peace-offering, for Liz planned to visit the actress that afternoon, quite possibly interrupting her in learning the lines of her latest play.

She hadn't bothered to change. Anne's own elegance was too awesome to emulate, and anyway Liz felt comfortable to live in shorts and bikinis, especially as with every day the heat and the light seemed to intensify in skies blazingly clear and blue.

There was a silver Mercedes parked in the lane near the villas, but Liz thought nothing of it. She knocked at Anne's door and waited, humming a happy little tune and looking forward to an afternoon chatting and laughing and keeping her thoughts off Hugh. So when the door opened to reveal a half-naked and astonishingly good-looking young man, Liz was ready to beat a hasty retreat. She must have picked the wrong house after all.

The young man seemed to like her shrunken tee-shirt. He grinned as he raised his eyes to her face. 'I hope I can help you,' he said, confident of his own appeal. His eyes, Liz noted with some alarm, were a blue you could only describe as electric. Striped Bermuda shorts outlined the muscular contours of lean hips and strong thighs, and a matt bronze tan covered every inch of his heroic physique. 'What can I do for you?' he asked again pleasantly, his smile revealing white teeth in a good-humoured face crowned by cropped golden curls which licked his temples like wavering flames.

Liz swallowed and found voice. 'I was looking for Mrs Leigh Bycroft,' she said uncertainly. 'My name is Elizabeth Larking.'

'Elizabeth?' Adonis frowned, then his fine brow cleared. 'Liz — of *course*! I remember now. Mother told me about you — the little nurse she met on the plane.' And before Liz could take umbrage in defence of her small stature, she found herself grabbed by the arm and hurried unceremoniously round to the back of the bungalow, her captor hissing that she was (for some extraordinary and incomprehensible reason!) the one girl in all the world he most wanted to meet. At that precise moment.

He dumped Liz on a garden bench and checked back over his shoulder to make sure they were not observed from the windows and the open patio doors. Richard Bycroft. Liz had worked this out for herself by the time this determinedly persuasive young man had got round to an explanation of his cavalier performance. Anne's son . . .

Liz was reluctantly impressed. Such a fascinating and expressive face; the face, one would have thought, of a born actor. If Richard truly *was* a hotel manager, however high-class his establishment — what a loss to the world of films where cameras might linger lovingly over such masculine beauty.

Satisfied they had not been seen, Richard collapsed on to the wooden seat with a groan of relief. One sharp glance at Liz was sufficient to warn him that this puzzled girl was harbouring feelings of annoyance likely to require the application of an immediate salve.

He sprang to his feet again, performed an elegant bow — and kissed her hand. 'Richard Bycroft,' he explained quite unnecessarily.

Liz was so taken aback she giggled. He was too affected for words — or rather his action was. Richard himself seemed nice. He grinned and sat down once more, confident he had not, after all, blotted his copybook. 'You must come and have dinner with me at my hotel. You know I'm manager at the Vicente?'

This was so sudden. They'd only known each other four and a half minutes! 'Your mother told me. It sounds a wonderful place.'

Impatiently Liz glanced at her watch. Was Richard making some kind of a pass at her? And where was Anne? Why had he hidden her in the garden and taken care to make sure they were out of sight of other eyes?

'Liz, my mother is ill! I've had to stay here the past couple of days to look after her. Fortunately the hotel's fairly quiet and my under-manager is a first-rate guy. But this time I think she's not going to recover as quickly.'

There was concern and compassion in the wide grey eyes now turned his way. But no surprise. 'You knew she was in poor health?' said Richard slowly, his own anxiety deepening. He and his mother were very close; his father had been dead the past ten years.

'I'm so sorry,' Liz replied carefully, not wishing to reveal those hints the actress had loosely dropped in their conversations. 'Working with sick people, one does develop a sixth sense and an eye for the smallest of signs. What does your doctor say?'

She watched the lean tanned hand, with its gold signet ring, rake that head of Byronic curls. 'I know it sounds the obvious thing to call in a doctor, but Mother is the most squeamish woman on the face of this earth. I tell you she's *paranoid* about doctors, won't have one near her. She even tells me there's nothing wrong — props herself upright on mounds of pillows and waits like some elegant ostrich for the trouble to go away of its own accord. And I have to admit she has got over these . . . these turns in the past.'

'Ah, I see.' Liz nodded thoughtfully. It all fitted now — the incident on the plane, the gloomy predictions delivered with false gaiety. The silly, brave woman. For it took a sort of upside-down courage to face sickness all on your own.

'Seeing you there on the doorstep — and remembering you're a nurse, I was suddenly struck by the thought that since Mother's taken such a shine to you, maybe she'd see sense if you talked to her, persuaded her she must seek help. There's this play in July at Chichester. She'd have to be fighting fit to take it on.'

'And she's in bed now?'

Richard nodded. 'She had a bad night again, though I think her breathing's improving. Of course she always sleeps bolt upright with masses of pillows, but last night I heard her crying out for air even though the windows were flung wide open.'

'Oh, Richard, come on!' Liz leapt to her feet, anxious to waste no more time. Anne might need oxygen cylinders bringing in; there must be something Liz could do to make her more immediately comfortable. 'Let's see what can be done.' Secretly she hoped to find the actress far less ill than her son suspected . . .

But the sight of Anne, propped up against her mound of pillows, flushed and frail and labouring for breath, brought little comfort. 'How are you, Anne?' asked Liz softly, closing gentle fingers over the thin wrist. 'I'm so sorry to find you under the weather. I brought you this,' she produced a pink marzipan shrimp, 'but it wasn't intended to be medicine.'

It was a feeble enough joke, but Anne struggled to lighten the atmosphere with a chuckle, the effort making her cough painfully. 'Let me straighten things up a bit.' Liz moved around the bed, smoothing sheets and plumping pillows, fetching a cool flannel and some eau-de-cologne; keeping her expression reassuring and compassionate while her sharp mind memorised all the clinical symptoms it could gather. 'You should have sent for me before,' she scolded gently. 'You know I would have come straightaway.'

'My dear child, I know also that you're not a free agent. And that employer of yours has the devil's own temper. Besides, there's nothing much wrong with me that a bit of rest won't sort out.'

'Mr Forsythe? I'm not afraid of him,' declared Liz stoutly. 'And I think you'd be surprised what a charmer he can be when he feels like it.' She avoided the quizzical light in Anne's sharp blue eyes, less brilliantly blue now than her son's, but still lovely in their way.

'You see, Richard!' challenged his mother. 'You don't after all have a monopoly on charm.' But she smiled lovingly all the same at her splendid son who, totally unabashed, bestowed on them both a grimacing tease of a wink. He went off to the kitchen to prepare a tray of iced drinks.

'Don't let Richard alarm you on my account,' said Anne immediately they were alone. 'These setbacks . . . they come and go.' She struggled to rear herself higher on the pillows, her shoulders heaving with a bubbling chesty cough.

Heavy dark rings of sleeplessness shadowed the fine eyes, contrasting with the hectic colour of her cheeks. Fever? wondered Liz, wishing Anne kept a thermometer in the house; taking the dry hot hand in hers and noting the texture and warmth of the skin.

'Do you always sleep with so many pillows?'

Anne attempted a feeble chuckle and patted her throat. 'Terribly bad for the chins, darling, I know. But I do need lots of air and it helps the breathing.'

'It's much worse when she lies flat,'

agreed Richard, carrying in glasses and a jug of iced lemonade. 'As though her lungs are filling up with fluid.'

Liz nodded understandingly, striving to conceal her very real concern.

Anne was pressing her fingers to her face, hiding her reddened cheeks. 'I hate being caught without my war-paint!'

'Really, Mother!' exclaimed Richard, exasperated. He went out of the room, leaving the two women alone together.

'Delicious!' approved Liz, sipping her iced lemon with relish. It was almost as good as Hugh's version. 'Now why don't I help you put your face on, if it makes you feel better. I can pass the things you need and hold the mirror for you.' She surveyed the lavish array of jars and bottles on Anne's dressing table. 'Now what shall I pass you first?'

'My green cream, darling. Hides a multitude of sins.'

Anne was speaking jerkily now as breathlessness took its toll. Before Liz's very eyes the green cream cancelled out the hectic flush; then, followed by a smoothing of expensive foundation in a cool matt beige, that exquisite complexion became recreated before Liz's wondering gaze. For the actress this procedure was mere routine, one of the tools of her trade.

When it was time to leave, Richard escorted Liz to the top of the dusty lane, expressing his relief and gratitude that she'd promised to enlist Mr Forsythe's expertise. 'You are truly the most wonderful girl, Liz.'

'It's not me you'll need to thank,' she responded straightly, determined not to succumb to Richard's ardent, admiring blue eyes. 'If anyone can help your mother it's a heart specialist. And Anne knows he's one of the top men in London. If that doesn't give her confidence then I don't know what will!'

She wasn't quick enough to prevent her small hand being captured and clasped against this charmer's beating heart. At least *he* sounded healthy enough, with that measured rhythmic throb. Liz controlled her lips with wry firmness, not wanting to spoil the moment with an out-of-place smile. Richard's anxiety was so patently genuine; this high-powered display was intended as a demonstration of his gratitude. Yes, he was an actor at heart.

'I can't begin to tell you what a comfort you're being to me,' he was insisting seductively, his eyes never leaving the heart-shaped face, dwelling upon her with such intensity Liz felt certain she must have a smut on her nose. Blatant charm was all very well, and Richard Bycroft was sensational to look at. But after living with a man like Hugh, young Bycroft was . . .

. . . just plain boring, thought Liz that night as she waited for the right moment to interrupt Hugh's reading. They were dining out — Hugh's suggestion. Nowhere smart, but a small place in Albufeira where Hugh said the fishermen themselves ate and the food was authentic and good. She had put on her pink dress and brushed her hair till it shone, tumbling in soft waves down to the slim golden shoulders. Then she changed her mind — lest it seemed she was aping Rosita's rich mane — and scraped the lot back in a ponytail. Now she sat quietly waiting, her own thoughts more absorbing than the unread magazine in her lap.

The evenings were getting lighter now. When Hugh could see to read no more he kept a watchful eye on Liz. 'You're very restless tonight,' he observed lazily, his eyes glittering in the distance, shadows emphasising the ruthless, sensual lines of his lean face. 'Are you about to tell me you want to go back to England early?'

Liz gasped and swallowed. What a dreadful, *impossible* idea! He could not be more wrong. She stuttered her protests, knowing she sounded gauche and inarticulate. But how to convince him without giving away the depth of her compulsive feelings where he was concerned? If Hugh should guess, she could not bear his scorn.

'Do you know Anne Leigh Bycroft?' she blurted out of the blue.

'Know *of* her. You sat next to her on that flight, didn't you? She has a villa somewhere round these parts. Penny once mentioned it.' A laconic hand gestured in recollection. 'Fine-looking woman. I saw her once on the London stage — Ibsen, I think it was. She was younger then, of course, and I was in my pre-clinical years at med school. We all found her devastatingly beautiful, even in early middle age. Similar looks, I suppose, to Vivien Leigh.'

'Mr Forsythe,' said Liz worriedly, leaning forward and clasping slim fingers till the knuckles whitened, 'Anne hates doctors.'

Hugh looked mystified, as well he might, and slightly hurt. 'So? She's not the first — and I'll hazard a guess she won't be the last.'

Damn it, she was expressing herself badly! 'Well, no — that's not what I mean exactly. Anne hates the thought of illness, the very idea of it. She's actually *frightened* of doctors and never goes to see one. The thing is — I believe she *is* ill and needs treatment.'

'Oh yes?' Hugh mustered up an expression of polite interest.

'I've got as detailed a case history as possible, from Anne herself and from her son, Richard Leigh Bycroft.'

At the mention of that name, it seemed to her the surgeon's face darkened briefly, though he made no further comment. It was possible, of course, that he had visited the Hotel Vicente in the past, with his wife Penelope, or with the Vedras couple, though Richard had given no intimation he might have met the surgeon already. 'I believe he calls himself Richard Bycroft,' she explained. 'He manages a hotel out here — '

'I know,' said Hugh shortly. 'However, I hadn't made the connection between that young man and Mrs Leigh Bycroft. Go on.'

Observing how his mouth had tightened into that cruel line, Liz fidgeted nervously with a tendril of hair escaping out of her ponytail. It was clear the surgeon considered it sheer temerity on her part to involve herself with another person's health, and then attempt to drag him into the business too!

And why not? her rebellious streak insisted. He had taken the Hippocratic oath, hadn't he? Did being a powerful surgeon put him above helping with more mundane problems? If indeed what was wrong with the actress should prove to be so.

Hugh continued to scowl at her. She looked about fifteen with her hair fixed that way. The idea of her becoming entangled with this Bycroft character was distinctly unappealing, she would be too inexperienced to cope with that sort of professional charmer.

Interpreting the black looks as impatience, Liz rapidly listed all she had observed and discovered that might help towards Hugh's clinical diagnosis.

Those gimlet eyes rested unwaveringly upon her throughout, the surgeon's clever fingers stroking his mouth and chin in meditative fashion.

'Is she well enough to travel to the Clinic for tests?'

'Only by ambulance. Though I shouldn't be surprised if she refused to go.'

'Then it might be as well for me to visit Mrs Leigh Bycroft at her home,' suggested Hugh — to Liz's surprised delight. She couldn't hold back the beam of relief and pleasure that spread over her whole face. 'It may help to put her at her ease if we meet informally. And if I turn up unannounced on her doorstep and deploy my fatal charm, there won't be time for her to work herself into a state.'

'Mr Forsythe! I could hug you!' Liz bounced up in her chair, clasping her hands in a spontaneous gesture of relief. He'd come up with the perfect solution to the thorny question of how to get Anne to the Clinic for examination — just what Liz would have prescribed, but hadn't dared suggest.

'Shouldn't do that if I were you,' growled the surgeon with a quirk of those wicked eyebrows. 'You might get a warmer reception than you bargained for, Miss Larking!'

Liz bit her lip and lapsed back into a more dignified frame of mind. His words rang in her ears, a warning not to overstep the bounds of familiarity. '*My fatal charm*' — he'd delivered that with an irony which made it quite clear Hugh Forsythe regarded charm in a man with contempt. Yet even if he did not realise it, he'd charmed her with the powerful thrall of his personality. And Liz had come to dread the days — even the hours — they were apart. A fascination far more fatal than Richard Bycroft's manufactured style.

Something guarded in his young companion's expression brought a mirthless bark of laughter from Hugh's throat. 'You'd better accompany me,

Nurse Larking, while I demonstrate that my bedside manner's as impeccable as my cutting technique. We'll take Mrs Leigh Bycroft by surprise, then. Tomorrow, at eleven.'

In the café on the cliffs, tucking into a local speciality, a savoury stew of pork and clams which came with a mound of golden chips and a salad rich with olive oil dressing, they discussed the day at the Clinic.

Until Hugh came up with a diagnosis of WPW syndrome, Kevin's case had all the doctors perplexed. Frequent fits of fainting and palpitations in a perfectly healthy young person who had no history of symptoms? Of course! The rare Wolff-Parkinson-White syndrome. There was the WPW pattern in the ECG print-out. Mother Flora and Dr Costa could have kicked themselves, but as Hugh pointed out with no false modesty, he had vast experience in cardiac problems and only one in ten doctors might be expected to pick up this one.

'I hope I'm not a cardiac consultant for nothing,' he chided in a goodhumoured attempt to rescue his mortified colleagues.

Liz and Hugh discussed this interesting case over their clams. 'Kev tells me you've promised he won't require surgery at the moment,' said Liz.

'That's right. Though one day a surgeon may decide to fit a pacemaker. This is an interesting dish, don't you think? Not to everyone's taste, but it's my particular favourite.' Hugh pushed the glistening salad away and went for a second helping of chips; tonight was a night for indulgence. Yesterday he'd been feeling like death — looked like it too, judging by the way everyone had handled him with kid gloves. Liz had seemed genuinely upset; no doubt about it, she was an exceptional girl, very caring. She would take any lame duck under her gentle wing. Why had he met her so late in life? She in her early twenties, he well on the wrong side of thirty. People would think he was mad, cradle-snatching . . .

'Strange it should only affect young people,' Liz said meditatively, chewing on a clam. She wasn't sure that she liked this unusual combination of meat and fishy food. The locals were knocking it back, though, with noisy relish. Nets hung from the low ceiling, their round glass floats almost ghostly in the muted light.

'It's caused by an abnormality of the heart's electrical pathway, often only discovered when we're doing a routine ECG.'

'How long must Kevin stay at the Clinic? He's chafing at the bit to be on his way, poor chap.'

'He can't leave till we've got the heartbeat regulated with drugs. It's these very fast beats which cause Kevin to faint — the WPW syndrome. My preference is for digitalis plus quinidine, but a patient's response can be unpredictable, so it's a case of trial and error till we get the most effective treatment . . . Don't look so anxious,

Liz, the prognosis is usually benign!'

'He's quite a dear, really,' said Liz with a grin. 'I've a soft spot for our Kev. He livens the world up a bit.'

'You've a soft spot for everyone, if you ask me.'

'And what's wrong with that?' she countered defensively. She could tell Hugh thought her a gullible girl from an over-sheltered background; but he was sufficiently familiar with the arduous training of nurses to know better! 'Anyway, that's not true,' she added firmly, meeting his black stare with a hostile eye. This image he appeared to have of her: naïve and simple-minded. Perhaps working at the Clinic would dispel the myth and he would appreciate her as another committed professional.

But Hugh was in too mellow a mood to care two hoots if little Liz felt hard-hearted towards him. He raised his glass and drank to her, a silent toast, and Liz was rocked by yet another of those disturbing, mysterious half-grins so freely in evidence once more. It was the old Hugh back again today, the weary stranger driven off by a whole uninterrupted night's rest. It was good to see, but uncomfortable all the same to be the object of that mocking surmise.

Liz squared her shoulders and drained her glass. Anne Leigh Bycroft's case on the morrow; it would be interesting to see how Hugh handled a patient even more nervous than most.

Later she was surprised to hear a knock at her bedroom door just as she was preparing for her bath. Too startled to respond, she heard the door open and Hugh — it must be Hugh! — come into the bedroom. Liz's heartbeat began to pound as her imagination raced away with itself. She wrapped a bath-towel round the parts that mattered and came timidly out of the bathroom, looking like a nervous Brigitte Bardot with her fair hair tumbling from its roughly tied topknot.

'I saw your light was still on and

I . . . ' Hugh was improvising rapidly. He should never have come barging into her room. 'I wanted to thank you.'

'Th-thank me?' Liz hitched at the towel which she'd suddenly discovered was not the bath size she'd thought but a rather meagre hand-towel.

'Yes,' said Hugh with an expansive gesture of the brandy glass in his right hand. Just to see her was inspiration. 'To thank you for holding the fort while I was away. And for helping out at the Clinic. Mother Flora was singing your praises with such fervour I got quite alarmed.'

'Al-alarmed?' Dash it, why couldn't she stop repeating his every last word? He must think she hadn't a brain in her silly head.

'I brought you back a present,' said Hugh, delving into his pocket and bringing out a small packet in gold wrapping. 'That stuff you wear will be okay in ten years' time. I'd prefer you in this. It's not so . . . seductive.'

A faint exasperation now tinged

Liz's bewilderment. A present — how thoughtful, though she'd done nothing to deserve one. The implied criticism — as if she'd set out to *vamp* the man! — was downright infuriating, never mind the practical difficulties when both hands were needed to maintain a decent dignity. 'Could you . . . would you mind putting it over there? I can't . . .'

'Of course,' muttered Hugh, dropping the packet on her pillow as if it burnt his fingers.

She hadn't said thank you! 'Thank you very much!' managed Liz faintly. 'I'll unwrap it when I've had my bath.'

'It's perfume. *Breath of Spring*. I like it.'

'Lovely!' breathed Liz. Go away, go away! her head screamed. I'm a mess. My mascara's running in the steam and my hair looks like a bird's nest. I don't want you to see me like this. It's not decent!

God, you are beautiful. Hugh stepped towards her and Liz tried to pass him. Whatever was he going to do?

She gasped aloud as his hands closed over her upper arms. Her knees were dissolving with panic and longing as she felt herself propelled towards the bed behind her, dimly aware of the mattress pressing against the back of her bare legs and her body sinking helplessly on to the knobbly cotton coverlet.

Then the moment was past as having moved her from his path Hugh strode on and into the bathroom, where he turned off the tap with an angry snarl.

'Thanks for taking all the hot water,' he observed sourly, coming out of the bathroom and frowning down at Liz, sprawling on the bed, her mouth agape with disbelief and chagrin.

'Good night, then. And don't be late up, I think I'll have an early cooked breakfast.'

# 7

'Still a most attractive woman . . . most attractive,' said Hugh thoughtfully as they left Anne's villa. Since he seemed to be talking to himself, Liz made no reply, but frowned and bit her lip. Jealous, are we? teased a mocking little imp inside her head. Don't be ridiculous, scolded the sensible part of her brain. The very idea!

'This way,' ordered Hugh, ignoring the homeward road and setting off purposefully in the direction of the beach. 'We'll take a walk. No need for me to leave till this afternoon. It's a glorious day — the air's like wine.' He inhaled great draughts, head thrown back, eyes screwed up to combat the brilliance of the cobalt skies. A stethoscope dangled incongruously from the pocket of his tailored linen jacket. He wasn't dressed for the beach, but it was typical of him not to care.

Meekly Liz swivelled on her heel and followed in Hugh's steps, towards an ocean of molten silver framed between the resinous clumps of tall dark pines. That commanding air of Hugh's, that assumption that he'd be instantly obeyed — once upon a time it made her hackles rise — but that was history nowadays. Liz simply wanted to be where Hugh was, to go where he was going. If he strode out to sea fully clothed, she'd be right behind him.

Hugh put on a pair of dark glasses with heavy black frames. They gave him a sinister air. He slowed his pace until Liz caught up. She was breathing rapidly, seemed already out of breath. He shortened his stride to accommodate hers.

'Your case history was a great help this morning — very thorough. I could use you in my Thursday afternoon clinic, if you've no other plans.'

Liz's beam of pleasure was answer

enough. But the credit was Hugh Forsythe's. He couldn't have been more skilful in his handling of this phobic patient. He hadn't, though, been particularly friendly where Richard was concerned, and Liz recalled the doctor's black scowl when she had first mentioned that Anne had a son living locally, by name of Richard Bycroft. It was a bit of a puzzle. Richard for his part had been sincerely grateful — and apparently unaware of any undercurrents of hostility. There'd been no indication of their meeting before, though it was quite conceivable the Forsythes might have dined in the past at the Hotel Vicente.

It had worked out just as Hugh predicted. There he was at her bedside — before Anne could realise what was going on and work herself into a state of anxiety. She was totally beguiled by finding such reassurance and quiet consideration displayed by a doctor she'd heard described as a man of storms. In fact Anne responded with meek and trustful acquiescence to every requirement Hugh stipulated. There was no time-wasting argument. Yes, she was already resigned to the prospect of surgery. And if Hugh could indeed operate at the Clinic, then she could avoid a return to London and the barrage of publicity that could damage her standing with producers and directors unwilling to risk working with a lame duck. Moreover, Richard was insisting that his mother convalesce in pampered luxury at the Hotel Vicente.

They were coming down now on to the beach. Liz slipped off her espadrilles, enjoying the sensation of silken sand slithering between her toes. Hugh was right: the sea air was heady as wine. They began to stroll along the water's edge and when Liz broke into a high-spirited joyous gambol, racing in and out of the shallows and splashing her boss, he responded goodhumouredly, outpacing her to the farthest rocks and turning to grab hold of her when she careered into him, tripping over her own feet and almost sending him headlong into the sea.

His long legs scaling the rocks, careless of his expensive linen suit, Hugh led the way up to the cliffs above. It was more of a clamber than a climb, for the cliffs were low and unsheer. Here grew grasses and wild flowers, even down to the water's edge. Gallantly he lent a hand to haul Liz up — she was so much smaller than he — until at last they were standing together on the ochre soil of the headland.

It was breathtaking — the rich orange earth patchworked with the intense pink and purples of mesembryanthemum daisies, clumps of white-flowered cistus turning their golden centres to the sun. The two of them strolled on until Hugh pointed out a patch of inviting shade, where a gnarled and wind-listed olive tree made an umbrella of shelter to rest beneath. Liz subsided gracefully on to the grassy spot, her flowered skirts spreading under her like unfolding petals. The air smelled wonderful, salt and fresh, yet sweet with a thousand scents. Taking off his jacket, Hugh slung it carelessly from a low branch, rolling up his sleeves and unbuttoning his shirt in the heat.

'Look,' he rested both hands on her shoulders, kneeling beside her on the grass, turning her body to face inland, 'you can see the Casa de la Paz, just beyond the clump of the pine trees.' His hands burned through the thin fabric of her white camisole blouse, making the flesh throb with the pulse of her blood. Even when he let her go, Liz could sense the imprint of his fingers marking her skin.

Hugh lay back, eyes closed behind the blank dark lenses of his sunglasses. Liz hardly dared to stare, yet she could not concentrate on the loveliness of the scenery. She was thinking of Hugh walking unannounced into her room, and herself so foolishly jumping to the conclusion that he'd come to — to —

His arms were folded behind his

head, the muscles taut and stretched. His throat, exposed by the open shirt, bronzed and strong yet strangely vulnerable. Liz felt a constriction in her chest, a cruel hand squeezing her heart. Her shoulders rose and fell rapidly with her breathing . . . If we stay here much longer, she reasoned wildly, I shall have to tell him what's happening to me — pour it all out of my system.

Pearls of sweat broke out on her forehead, and, feeling their coldness, she wiped them away with the back of her hand. Frantically she made an effort to pull herself together and stop behaving like an infatuated schoolgirl. She tore a daisy out of the grass and mindlessly attacked it, petal by petal. 'What exactly is wrong with Anne, Mr Forsythe?'

He took his dark glasses off the better to see her. 'I think you know me well enough by now to use my Christian name. This scrupulous courtesy is making me feel like your grandfather!'

'Sorry.' Darting a sidelong glance,

she saw he was grinning at her, and it softened the sarcasm she heard in his voice. He clamped a blade of grass between his lips, propping himself on one elbow and gazing out to sea as he contemplated her question. His teeth, she saw, were very white, slightly irregular, the eye-teeth small and pointed and feral.

Liz sat and hugged her knees. 'I thought it must be a legacy from that childhood rheumatic fever.' She plucked another flower and began removing each petal. He loves me . . . he loves me not . . . he loves me . . .

'Absolutely,' said Hugh, seeing the little game she was playing, the age-old rhyme. He guessed Liz's mind was less concerned with the condition of Anne Leigh Bycroft's heart valves than with that rake of a son.

To get away from Hugh's coolly speculative gaze, Liz sank down flat on the grass and buried her face in her arms. Now that Anne was definitely Hugh's case, she didn't wish to overstep the bounds of curiosity; all the same, she was anxious to know what the surgeon had discovered during his careful and thorough examination.

Hugh burned with irritation. What a picture of love-sickness! An illness he was totally unqualified to cure, however much he empathised with those symptoms clearly tearing Liz apart. Noiselessly he ground his teeth. He'd seen the way Bycroft looked at her. That heartbreaker! Was no woman able to resist his calculated seductions? Hugh's mouth twisted with wry scorn. He forced his attention back to the case of Anne Leigh Bycroft. 'Living abroad, rheumatic fever in her early teens, parents unable to get hold of proper treatment for her — small wonder her heart became damaged! Fifty per cent of those contracting rheumatic fever suffer subsequent heart disease.

'Now, Liz, come on. What does that suggest to you? A condition affecting the heart valves. You must have nursed on cardiac wards.'

Liz rolled on to her back and found herself fearfully close to Hugh, looking up into his brooding face as he loomed over her, balancing his weight on one elbow. She could smell that lemony soap he used each morning in the shower after his swim. That sensual mouth was but inches above her own. If only he might want to lean down and kiss her! A strange languor stole through her limbs, even while she managed a perfect textbook definition of mitral stenosis.

'Good girl!' His breath as he spoke fanned her cheeks. 'And the breathless-ness is caused by a build-up of fluid in the lungs when in the prone position.'

Not in my case! considered Liz in alarm. How close were they both to the cliff edge? She stretched out her right hand and checked the solid ground.

'The reddened cheeks,' Hugh was murmuring, 'the motor flush. Irregular pulse.'

He was staring at her so intensely Liz

felt her heart miss a beat. Exactly her own symptoms! Might Hugh be going to . . . his face was so near . . . there was an extraordinary tenderness in those laser-black eyes.

Hugh sat up quickly. 'You any good at interpreting electro-cardiograms?' he questioned, brusquely disguising that momentary weakness. Couldn't he just picture it! — shock, horror, utter disbelief that her employer could have harboured such ideas about her. If only he could put back time, make himself young and full of hope again, as Liz now was, before the lessons of life had injected their measure of cynicism.

The magic moment was over. 'The nurse who does my ECGs is a good soul, but she's not all that efficient. And as you know, the quality of read-out is operator-dependent. She calibrates them manually and there's so much interference I hardly dare rely on them overmuch for my decisions.'

Liz sat up and hid her disappointment in a show of bright, intelligent interest. Her act was better than she knew. Hugh took it as evidence of relief at dealing with him in his safe professional role once more.

'I suppose that must mean you have to do your own if you want strict accuracy. You can hardly have the time — '

'Hell, no!' interjected the surgeon, stretching out at full length and looking, in his expensive casuals, about as hard-pressed as some continental playboy. 'I'm much too lazy for *that*. Anyhow, it's been so long since I had to do ECGs, I've probably forgotten how! No, Liz, if your efforts are more successful it will be an enormous help to me. You understand what I'm looking for — direct information about electrical currents within the heart muscle, specifics, rate and rhythm, conduction of impulses. I can then estimate whether there's any abnormality in the valves or in the size of the ventricles.'

'Determine the degree of ventricular

hypertrophy and decide whether there's valvular stenosis or incompetence — simply by studying the ECG. Yes, I see.' Brow furrowed in concentration, her mind racing ahead, Liz recalled that Hugh had got straight on the telephone and organised a private nurse to come and special Anne for a few days before admitting her to the Clinic for the necessary tests. Here was Liz's chance to help. 'Can I do Anne's ECG for you? Would you trust that to me?'

'Far better than subjecting her to the ministrations of total strangers when she's so apprehensive . . . ' Hugh flapped a lazy hand to discourage a trio of persistent gnats hovering inches above his nose.

He closed one eye and tilted his head in a determined effort to be objective. But it was no good. Whichever way you chose to look at her, Liz Larking was a dream come true. All things bright and beautiful. Her only flaw was a determination to underrate herself — oh, *and* that fixation with health food! Bycroft wouldn't go much for that one: he struck Hugh as the sort of man who liked his steaks rare and his women overdone. Like Rosita! The thought of Liz succumbing to Bycroft's practised seduction was unbearable.

Liz just sat and glowed with pride. She'd never been a mind-reader. Fancy Hugh Forsythe trusting her with such responsibility! Asking her to help with case histories and with the ECGs. Here was her chance to show him the determined, professional side of Liz Larking, instead of that crazy, emotionally-disturbed idiot who had surfaced out there in Portugal. She could do ECGs. There were twelve different variations of squiggle, and these must be interpreted as accurately as possible. The procedure itself was not difficult. As for the case histories — this required human qualities of empathy, drawing from the patient the smallest detail, however apparently trivial, encouraging their trust and confidence.

She sat there, brushing bits of grass off her skirt and smiling happily to herself at the prospect of being useful and working with Hugh. 'You are a surprising girl!' he suddenly exclaimed right out of the blue.

Liz just couldn't help herself, couldn't hold back her instant response. The words formed themselves of their own accord, taking the man and the woman equally by surprise. Her voice was low and enigmatic, even sullen. 'There's a lot about me that would surprise *you*, Mr Forsythe.'

They were both standing now, Hugh reaching for his jacket, raising an arm to mask that probing gaze with dark-lensed sun-specs. In silence he studied the averted profile. She would not meet his eye. For one shattering moment he wondered if he'd been mistaken. But the closed face, pale beneath its tan, was giving no clues away to help him figure out the truth. Foolish child! Did she think he was blind, then? It was pathetically easy to guess the name of that fellow playing havoc with her heart.

'You must know, Liz, that I feel responsible for you while you're under my roof. I know you don't want my advice, but just remember this is a temporary situation. There's another life to consider back home.'

There was no telling how long she'd been involved in this affair with Bycroft, but the looks that had passed between them told quite a story: cool nonchalance on Liz's part, utter confidence on his.

Rage swept through the doctor. With harsh fingers he gripped her chin and forced her to meet his stern black eyes. But she wrenched her head away and stepped back against the narrow trunk of the wind-warped olive, perilously close to the cliff's edge. Hugh was being cruel to be kind, he had guessed her feelings. He needed her help but he didn't want her love. He was warning her that it was just foolish infatuation and he wasn't the sort of man to take advantage of a silly girl offering her heart on a plate. The only hearts *he* was interested in came shrouded in sterile towels and presenting fascinating and curable problems for him to solve, with his knife and with his brain.

Her awful secret was discovered.

Liz sank down to find her espadrilles, eyes swimming, fingers searching blindly. When Hugh reached out a hand to help her keep her balance she ignored him and clung instead to the tree's rough bark. She paced down the pathway ahead of him, a sweating, dusty hand smearing away the tears that seared her eyelids in a pretence of shielding off the knowing rays of the watching sun.

Next morning when a delivery boy rode his motor scooter up the drive of the Casa de la Paz, it had to be Hugh who was crossing the hall and who answered the doorbell.

'For you, I believe,' he said grimly, handing Liz the gift-wrapped sliver of crystal containing one perfect red rosebud, red as blood in the pulsating depths of its crimson heart. For her part Liz was only too miserably aware how careful he was that his fingers should not touch hers. 'That can't be for me.' She shook her head in angry denial though the gilt-edged card said otherwise. 'I don't want it!'

Hugh's voice struck chill. 'You strange little thing,' he observed with a wondering shake of his head. For a lovesick girl she was putting on a lousy act today, wandering about as though her world had collapsed. Then when the love-token that should have set her on top of the moon arrived, she looked fit to weep with misery. The trouble with Liz Larking, she was too attractive for her own good.

He peered across her shoulder at the dramatic italic script. 'Elizabeth — with eternal gratitude. My love — Richard.' He saw how the delicate rosebud quivered in her fingers, eternal symbol of a captivated heart. Whose heart? considered Hugh with weary cynicism. Not that scoundrel's for a start. And what other services might the girl have already rendered to deserve the reward of that one perfect bloom? The idea so infuriated him that he could have reached out and destroyed that insinuating little message with ruthless pleasure . . .

With a start of surprise he realised that was exactly what Liz was doing, her fingers deliberate and rock-steady as they ripped the card to shreds and cast it into the waste bin along with the vegetable peelings. At the hiss of Hugh's audible exasperated sigh she turned to look up at him in some curiosity, noting the weary gesture of incomprehension he made with his hands, palms turned upward and outward, echoing the tone of his voice. 'I just can't fathom you, you fickle-hearted, romantic girl. You ought to be over the moon, making such a conquest!'

Not waiting for an answer, he swung on his heel and strode across the kitchen, while Liz, stunned and speechless, glared daggers at his departing back. 'I — I — ' she stuttered, her tongue cleaving dryly to the roof of her mouth. 'I hate you!' was all she could think of to hurl after him.

At the doorway Hugh swung round and looked at her.

'I hate you!' she cried again, wishing with all her heart that were true.

The surgeon grinned at her mirthlessly, his eyebrows quirked in pretended outrage at such rebellion. 'Yes,' he observed imperturbably, 'but you *love* hating me too. Wouldn't you say so?'

He stamped away and closeted himself in his study. To clear her head and work some of the tensions out of her system, Liz walked to the shops instead of taking the car. It was a bit of a trek, but she needed to get out on her own and put a bit of space between herself and Hugh. He was getting so grumpy lately, and she was at a loss to find a reason for it. Luisa was vacuuming, Liz was best out of the way.

On her return she unpacked the provisions and stowed them in larder and fridge, then changed into her bikini and did thirty lengths of the pool. Hugh was in his study. Strains of *The Art of Fugue* played on a harpsichord reverberated on the still, late-afternoon air. Luisa had abandoned her housework and was hosing the plants in the garden, a scarf tied over her straw hat, sunglasses perched on her nose.

Liz was floating dreamily on her back when out of the blue depths beneath her the sharklike figure struck. She was hoisted bodily clear of the surface and into the air, with a great whoosh of turbulence and her own voice screaming out in alarm. Luisa, hearing the cry, looked down towards the pool and saw the two figures thrashing about in the water, smiled and waved an untroubled hand. Dr Hugh and Senhorita Liz. He had seemed angry these past few days; to see him enjoying himself now — ah! but that was good. She laughed aloud, sharing their fun as Liz, held aloft on the doctor's brawny arms, was dropped into the water with a splash that soaked a cane lounger near the edge of the pool.

Fear and fury chased one another as Liz surfaced. What the devil was this beastly man up to now? There she'd been, quietly minding her own business. It was enough to give anyone a heart attack! Hugh of all people shouldn't take such risks. Liz opened her mouth to make vociferous protest . . . but where was he? A dark shape circled her, reaching for her legs. She tried to dodge, too late! and their bodies were thrashing and struggling in the churning waters, Hugh capturing her by the waist and hooking a ruthless leg between hers as they sank together to the bottom of the deep end.

Two could play at that game. Liz by now had her nerve back and she wriggled and twisted to outwit, with her slight and supple form, his effortless strength. She made herself slippery as an eel . . . went limp as a frond of becalmed seaweed . . . pulled him with her to the bottom in a test of endurance

. . . and finally dragged herself to the edge of the pool, exhausted. 'Pax!' she implored between huge gulps of air as Hugh lunged for her yet again. 'Pax — I'm half drowned!'

His eyes were wicked as he reared up like some great sea monster, blocking out the sun with the breadth of his shoulders, flexing the muscles in his arms and back as he reached for her, seal-wet and dangerously laughing. 'In that case, I'd better administer the kiss of life . . . '

Nervously Liz glanced round for Luisa, but she must have gone to water the Madonna lilies by the front door. Her eyes danced with mischief. 'You just dare,' she teased in breathless, simulated outrage. 'You just dare!'

Hugh spun out the tension, inching fractionally closer. But he'd waited too long. Liz had dived between his legs and was steaming across the pool, lifting herself out of the water and slithering on to the tiled surround. Saved by the skin of my teeth from a fate worse than death! she thought. She laughed and shivered at one and the same time, gooseflesh roughening her skin as she escaped to her bedroom. Hugh was in a playful mood, but he didn't know his own strength, that was for sure. Why, he'd almost drowned her like a helpless kitten!

At least he's coming out of that morose shell, she assured herself. Nothing to do with her, of course. Problems with his research could be getting him down. Still, he'd sort them out with that brilliant brain of his — had already done so, by the looks of things.

In the distance she thought she heard the faint ring of the telephone; Hugh would answer it; such calls were infrequent at the Casa.

Liz shed her wet bikini and wrapped herself in a bath-towel. Crossing to the bathroom, she blinked and hesitated, a frown creasing her forehead as she saw where someone — and certainly it could not be Hugh — had placed that fateful rose on top of the white chest of drawers. The heat of the day had begun to unfurl the delicate petals protecting its blood-red heart; the tough stem had lost a little of its stiffness and drooped with a rather graceful air of sadness at the coolness of its reception into the House of Peace.

Such a beautiful thing. Liz felt a twinge of compunction as her feet were drawn irresistibly across the polished floor. It was cruel to spurn such innocence solely because — as Hugh Forsythe had observed — the sender might be smitten. Unwelcome though the prospect might be. And very hard to believe. If the rose represented anyone's heart Liz had a tremulous suspicion it could well be her own . . . her throat ached and her fingers went out involuntarily to stroke those satiny petals.

A tap on the window caused her to start from her reverie. Her head swung round, wet snakes of hair whipping about her bare shoulders; slender fingers tightened their hold on the towel wrapped about her like a sarong. It was Hugh.

He opened the doors and stepped into the room, his eyes flickering down to the floor where her discarded bikini lay between them. 'I — er — I was just going to take a shower,' said Liz nervously, her gaze shying away from his.

'I've had a last-minute invitation to dine out. I just wanted to check with you first in case you've already bought stuff in.'

Liz made a brave attempt at a big bright uncaring smile. 'Of course not. Everything will keep in the fridge for another day.' I shan't miss you, Mr Forsythe. I shan't be counting the minutes till you're home.

I saw you, you little fool — lovingly caressing that flower you claim to spurn, secretly gloating over your 'conquest'. You're bright enough too, aren't you? Keeping your romance dark in case your family discover what games you've been playing under these seductive Algarve skies. Well, you're over

226

twenty-one and I'm not going to *keep* warning you you'll get hurt if Bycroft's playing true to form.

'I'll be out then, tonight,' Hugh reminded her, watching intently for the give-away gleam of pleasure; as soon as his back was turned she'd be on the phone to her lover. His eyes swivelled grimly to the flower she sheltered from his gaze, placing herself defensively in front of it.

He noted with sardonic amusement how she shielded that damn flower with her body. With studied insolence his black stare lingered on her scarlet cheeks, travelled to the rose behind her shoulder, compared the quality of their colour.

Liz ached for him to leave her room. Her thoughts were all confusion with him looming over her like Neptune, unconcernedly dripping puddles all over the polished parquet. Eyeing her with that blatant curiosity . . .

What if Hugh had changed his mind and decided he might enjoy a bit of dalliance after all? How cruelly humiliating! She simply could not bear it. Fists closed in torment, nails digging into her palms, Liz darted wild eyes about the room, seeking salvation from this hopeless situation.

And there it was — the answer to a desperate prayer.

She reached out for the one red rose and lifted the bloom to her face, inhaled deeply with closed eyes, fingers caressing that velvet softness. Then she opened her eyes and bestowed on Hugh a challenging, defiant stare.

He looked down his disdainful, arrogant nose, contemptuous of this girl and her 'lover'. And he must, as ever, have the final word.

Liz buried her face in the flower and her ears burned as hotly as her cheeks.

'Roses are full of earwigs,' said Hugh unromantically. 'Give you a nasty nip, earwigs.' And with a snort of derisive laughter he strode from the room, only the crash of the door behind him equalling the crescendo of his temper.

# 8

Liz busied herself lifting off the wires connecting each of Anne Leigh Bycroft's hands and feet to the machine. A fifth lead centred on the area of her heart, and Liz removed that one too. The actress smiled wanly up into the absorbed face bending over her. 'You were quite right, Liz. I'm just an old silly — that was nothing to get worked up about.'

Liz gave the thin fingers a conspiratorial squeeze and looked across to Hugh Forsythe. In his hands he held a thin strip of graph paper which he was studying with close attention, considering the message hidden in those vital squiggles.

'Good one,' he pronounced with satisfaction. 'I knew I could rely on my Liz.'

*His* Liz turned a delicate shade of poppy and dipped her head to conceal the involuntary smile of pride and pleasure. Hugh headed purposefully for the door. As he passed, he reached out a casual hand and patted her shoulder with a crisp, 'Well done!'

'What did he say?' asked Anne drowsily. An earlier session with the physiotherapist had left her quite exhausted.

'Let's get you back to your room,' suggested Liz with gentle solicitude. 'The physio's worn you out. And you're booked for another session with her tomorrow morning.'

Glowing with satisfaction that her technical skills had indeed been up to scratch, Liz wheeled Anne along the corridor to Room Three. The door was right opposite Room Ten and through the small observation window she could see Hugh, standing in silent contemplation and gazing down on the patient in the bed. Man or woman, Liz did not know. What she did know was that Hugh's approval had filled her with a lovely warm glow, and that Anne's

ECG had turned out as accurate as human hand could make it.

'Come and have lunch with me, Liz,' pleaded Mary, who never tired of listening to tales of Liz's own hospital experiences. 'D'you know I spent three hours last night on revision! After working here all day. Wasn't that noble? Just think, back to school proper next week, worse luck. Easter hols are over now.'

They linked arms and set off for the dining room. 'Gosh, we shall all miss you, Mary,' mourned Liz, racking her brain for fresh anecdotes to entertain her young companion over lunch. So much had happened since Finals. The General seemed light years away. They were on to the pudding before Liz brought up what was really on her mind. That nagging curiosity like a lingering toothache: Mr Forsythe and the patient in Room Ten.

'When you were setting up that mouth-care tray the other day, Mary. Was it for Room Ten?'

Mary nodded over a spoonful of fruit salad.

'Is that patient . . . a woman?' Liz was tense with anticipation, and the girl's affirmation brought a chill dampness to her clenched palms. Two-hourly mouth care. This woman must be very ill indeed — unable to do anything for herself, perhaps beyond communication.

Hugh Forsythe came surging into the dining-room, white coat flapping with the energy of his stride. He made for the table where Mother Flora and Dr Costa were deep in discussion. With such thoughts going through her mind, Liz could scarcely bear to look at him. Should he suspect she had guessed, what would there be to say? No crime had been committed. No wrong had been done. Except in Liz's own unmanageable heart . . .

'I don't know her real name,' Mary was saying, 'but the Sisters call her their Little Flower. They're so sweet to her, even though she's in a coma and never speaks or properly looks at us. They really love her. Although patients don't generally stay at the Clinic long-term, she's been here ages. By the way, Liz, did you see Kevin before his discharge? He specially wanted to say goodbye.'

Liz managed a weak smile. 'We're all invited to stay with his mum in Sydney, Australia. I should think she'll have a fit if anyone takes Kev up on it!'

'Forgive the interruption, ladies.' Hugh had both hands on the back of Mary's chair and was leaning over her head. 'I just wanted to check. You are free to give me a hand this afternoon, aren't you, Liz?' He was smiling down into Mary's adoring upturned eyes. 'How about you too, blossom?'

Joy and dismay chased themselves across the teenager's vivid face. Liz veiled her own expression with drooping lashes. What it must be like to allow your eyes to express your feelings with such innocent betrayal . . . a dangerous game when those eyes were linked by a hotline to an aching and vulnerable heart.

'I promised Sister Cecilia I'd tidy some stock cupboards for her, then she was going to teach me how to do injections. Not on real people,' Mary added hastily, lest Mr Forsythe get the wrong idea. 'We're using a piece of sponge, I think.'

'Much more valuable than doing a bit of clerical work for me.' He was focusing on Liz now. 'So long as I've got you.' It echoed in her brain . . . so long as I've got you, so long as I've got you . . .

'My Outpatients' Clinic starts at one-thirty. You'll find they're mainly heart patients today as I have such limited time available for consultation. As each patient arrives, I'd like you to interview them and write me up as detailed a case history as you can elicit.'

That evening on the way home in Hugh's Renault they discussed together the day's work. 'I was most impressed that you picked up the man with the white ring around the eye pupils,' said Hugh. 'It speeds things up for me no end if I've got a decent case history to start on. Nurses today are so highly trained; in some areas you know almost as much as medical students.'

Steeling herself to ask, and well aware that she must guard against the temptation to become over-involved emotionally with the case, Liz put the question of Anne's diagnosis. 'I suppose you are going to have to operate?'

Hugh nodded. The car windows were fully wound down and the orange groves they drove through gave off a perfume of incredible sweetness. Globes of ripe fruit glowed among the scented white of the flowers like thousands of orange suns. Hugh had explained how the trees bore their fruit, alongside the flowers for the next crop, in miraculous abundance.

'I'm scheduling Anne for Tuesday. Blood is building up in her lungs because of the mitral stenosis. You see, the blood can't get through the heart on its way from the lungs to the rest of the body. It pools in the lungs. So, Liz, surgery is our only solution. Your ECG confirms my judgment that we must open up the stenosed valve and let the blood get through freely.'

The road sign ahead warned PERIGO. Hugh slowed and took the narrow hump-backed bridge at a more judicious speed. 'You may care to act as scrub nurse with the team. Don't go round fainting in theatre, do you?'

Liz was trying to picture the scene, with herself a reluctant participant. 'Not as a general rule,' she said, recalling a bit of a shaky start in her first venture into the world of surgery. 'But I've never seen an operation on someone personally known to me. Can I have time to think this one over . . . ?'

\* \* \*

Sister Cecilia, head of the cheerful nursing team, wasted no time but tackled Liz next day about the scheduled mitral valvotomy. 'When it's one of H.F.'s ops. I always scrub for him. Some of our younger people find him a mite awesome in theatre — but I tell 'em he's a lovely man if you don't let him smell the fear.' She had such an infectiously wicked chuckle that Liz just had to join in; these nuns certainly had the measure of Hugh Forsythe. Fearing no man and loving all, surgeon of eminence or down-and-out bottom of the pile.

'Now would you mind acting as runner? I shouldn't suggest it if you were an actual relative, of course. But you don't look the sort of lass to turn squeamish just because the patient happens to be a friend. And I'm sure you'd be interested to see H.F. at work.'

'Yes, I can certainly cope with that,' agreed Liz with smiling assent. A runner did not have to scrub with the rest of the surgical team, but was designated the 'dirty' nurse, handling the unsterile and used equipment that the 'clean' staff must not touch. She would see Hugh operate, without getting in his way or playing an intrusive part in the action.

Mother Flora's head peered round Sister's door. The little office was right next to the OT entrance. 'Mary wanted to borrow this,' she said, holding up a paperback with a white cover and bold red-lettered title. 'Does anyone know where she might be?'

'Mother, could you hang on a moment? About the instruments for the valvotomy — do you suppose H.F. plans to use that new toy of his?' Sister detained Liz with a gentle hand. 'Mary is sitting in Room Ten doing some revision. Perhaps you'd be a kind lass and pop Mother Flora's book along to her.'

'Gladly,' said Liz, aware of an unusual frisson of apprehension even though she had been handed a legitimate reason for seeing Room Ten for herself. Cautiously she opened the door and sure enough, there was Mary in the easy chair by the window, her veiled white head bent in rapt concentration over a file of handwritten notes and diagrams. 'Biology,' she whispered as Liz raised questioning eyebrows. 'A Levels in June.'

Now she was there Liz found she didn't want to look at the bed. She had caught a quick glimpse of complicated machinery and a slight, motionless shape beneath the blue coverlet, harnessed to these contraptions by a series of leads and wires. She was reacting, she realised, as a layman must when faced with the trappings of intensive care — she who had already spent months working and using the very machines that now seemed awesome and alien.

She had to force herself to complete her errand, speaking in a low murmur so as not to disturb the sick woman; for of all the senses, hearing remained acute even in the dying, and a nurse must at all times guard her tongue lest she cause unnecessary distress. 'Mother sent this.' She handed Mary the copy of *Psychology as Applied to Nursing*. 'She suggests you look at Chapters Two and Three on student nurses in training.'

'Thanks, Liz. I like to sit in here with the Little Flower and get on with my work. It's so peaceful. The hum of the machines doesn't bother me at all. After all, they're keeping this poor lady alive.'

Together they approached the bedside, compassionate eyes upon the comatose patient. However many times she witnessed this spectacle Liz found it awesome to contemplate another human being, suspended between life and death, linked by a breathing tube to the bulk of the ventilator. And it struck her anew, the contrast between the pale lifelessness of the face, the stillness and quietness of that narrow shape beneath the coverlet, and the intrusive clatter of the ventilator. This woman . . . who *was* she?

No, in all truth Liz could not say she found this room a peaceful place. Poor thing! She looked . . . quite young, though the fleshless face made it difficult to pinpoint her age. Thirties, perhaps. The skin was sallow and stretched over the frail bone structure, the mouth partially obscured by the breathing tube, the hair cropped short for comfort and ease of care. In the winter, said Mary, Sister had knitted a little cap of fine baby wool.

Liz shuddered and sought refuge in the practicality of showing Mary how to use a small suction tube to clean the breathing tube of the thick secretions that accumulated. All the time the woman's eyes remained not quite closed, a faint line of white showing beneath translucent purple-veined lids.

Then, that small task completed, Liz moved back to the window and stared out over the courtyard, her eyes resting on the low building of the small Chapel. 'Who is she?' Her throat was so dry the question was incomprehensible. She swallowed, and asked again, 'Who is she?'

Mary had noticed nothing strange.

'You'll have to ask Reverend Mother about that. There's no name on the charts to go by, but then they never leave this room. Mr Forsythe comes in to see her several times a day when he's here at the Clinic. Honestly, Liz, this lady gets wonderful care. There isn't anything more the doctors could do.'

'Her body . . . are there scars of burns, or other injuries?'

Mary shook her head, puzzled at the expression in Liz Larking's troubled face. 'Sister told us it's a case of irreversible brain damage. I guess it must have been a stroke.'

With a great effort Liz pulled herself together and managed a convincing but tremulous smile. 'I'm sorry, Mary. Sorry, I mean, to have interrupted your work. I'll leave you and your Little Flower in peace.'

That night in the darkness of her curtained bedroom Liz tossed and turned, racked with anguish at the thought that the patient in Room Ten might indeed be Hugh's wife. Not in fact dead . . . but, and Liz trembled to think of it, so gravely injured that she must lie there in the Clinic, a sleeping princess, lovingly tended to the end of her unnatural days. Liz sat up and pummelled her pillow in bitter dismay. That poor creature Hugh's *wife?* But it would explain why he stole into Room Ten and stood in graven silence, gazing down on the living shell of his once-lovely Penelope. And that warning he'd given Liz, when in her eyes he read the truth of her love for him, high on the cliffs in the sunshine and among the profusion of wild flowers. His words — how was she ever to erase them from memory? — had reminded her that there was another, and separate, life for them both back home. Under his roof and his protection . . . ah yes, she hadn't comprehended anything more than the pain of rejection. But if his wife *was* alive and in this tragic condition, then yes, Liz understood.

Eyes straining painfully against the darkness, Liz had a flash of grim inspiration. It made her shudder even to dream of doing such a thing, but the proof might lie under this very roof. In Hugh's study . . . surely there must be, somewhere, a picture, a photograph of Penelope?

Even during those days alone at the Casa, Liz hadn't ventured alone into Hugh's private domain. Except just that once, to take the file on his desk and deliver it to the Clinic. And she'd done *that* with such haste she hadn't stopped to look. It was no good that prickly conscience reminding her she was intruding into matters that were none of her concern. 'I just have to know,' she wept into her unhelpful pillow. 'I just *have* to know. If I'm right, then it'll break my heart. And if I'm wrong . . . '

★ ★ ★

Anne lay supine on the black cushions of the operating table, the round circles of the theatre lights directed upon her unconscious body. Green-clad figures moved purposefully back and forth, shrouding the recumbent form with sterile towels, guiding instrument trolleys into position, while the anaesthetist, a nervy little Portuguese, checked over his patient's level of consciousness.

An outward picture of calm serenity in her white dress and white theatre clogs, Liz waited with bated breath for the surgeons to appear. The anaesthetist was continually darting uneasy glances towards the door Hugh would walk through. Scrub Sister's eyes twinkled kindly at him above her mask, as she passed a general comment that Mr Forsythe seemed in excellent humour that day. Liz, in her state of acute awareness, felt a lift in the atmosphere and joined in the evident sigh of relief.

The doors swung open. In strode two figures, almost comical in juxtaposition, one so tall, the other so short, yet both exuding a tangible sense of eagerly raring to go. H.F. and Mother Flora, unrecognisable in theatre caps and gowns. Like magnets Liz felt her eyes drawn to the taller surgeon, recalling the lines of that familiar body beneath the green operating garb. The very air was electric with his impatient vitality. Confidence irradiated him like a halo, and Liz's throat ached with pride. But she forced herself to stop gawping like a raw recruit and concentrate on playing an efficient, if insignificant, part of the action.

For one moment the calm black eyes met hers, then they swung to fix upon the anaesthetist on his high stool.

Mother Flora gave a little nod. 'Are we ready, Dr da Silva?'

The little man's eyes were wary again. He hitched his stool closer to Anne's head, as if her defenceless figure might afford some protection, and pulled his machinery right up to the end of the table.

Liz was concentrating on the deft hands of Mother Flora, her swift decisive movements as she assisted Mr

Forsythe. Mother Flora, she too a surgeon ... a scalpel stroked swiftly across the small square of exposed skin under which lay Anne's unsuspecting heart. The thin red line began to bleed gently, and suddenly Liz felt sick. Cold perspiration broke out on her forehead and she looked away. The bag on the anaesthetic machine puffed gently, in and out, in and out. The rhythm helped to calm her and she pulled herself together. Much safer to forget it was Anne who lay there. Concentrate on the consummate skill bent on healing her friend before her very eyes.

'Sucker!' muttered Hugh. Mother Flora moved in with the sucker and drew blood away from the open wound, allowing a clear field in which to work. So far the atmosphere was serenely efficient, the two surgeons communicating in a sort of shorthand of phrases and clipped sentences. So far ... Liz heaved a long breath ... so good.

Mother Flora was using retractors to hold back the friable edges of the wound, gently so that the vulnerable flesh would not be damaged. 'What do you think then of this job?' Hugh asked her, changing now to a scalpel with an adjustable blade. 'See how it virtually cuts round corners. This joint here — ' he demonstrated the technique ' — can be set at any angle and locked into position. Gone are the days when I had to bend my scalpels to operate on heart valves. Brilliant invention.'

Sister Cecilia spoke up with a quiet firmness and for the first time Liz noticed a trace of Scots accent. 'That swab can still be used, Mr Forsythe. They're too expensive to waste.'

Liz gasped and froze in anticipation of explosion. She dared not glance in Hugh's direction. The anaesthetist looked ready to dive behind his machine for cover. Sister Cecilia and Mother Flora worked on serenely.

'Quite right, Sister!' came the amazing reply. Hugh continued to use the offending swab until it was well and truly soaked with blood. 'Diathermy, please. And let's have some music.'

They were all looking now at her, Liz suddenly realised with a flush of chagrin. She'd been miles away, pondering over the meek display she had just witnessed. 'A cassette, Liz, if you would be so kind,' repeated Hugh with a mocking gleam in his wickedly black eye above the concealing mask. 'What would you like, Mother F.?'

They bent over Anne's opened-up chest discussing the options. Hugh wanted Bach's St John Passion, but Mother Cecilia considered this liturgically out of order since Easter was now past. So they settled for the B Minor Mass instead. Hugh grumbled a bit about 'everyone operating to this one nowadays', but seemed happy enough to hum tunelessly along with the huge choruses.

Liz was going to change the tape over when she noticed Hugh's forehead was a priority case, in danger of dripping sweat into the gaping wound. With a paper towel she mopped his broad and furrowed brow. 'You may not know this, Liz,' he said in didactic tones, 'but mitral valvotomy was the first operation ever done on the human heart, by the illustrious Lord Brock of Guy's. Of course, most of his early patients died. But he was sure enough of the logic of the operation to continue until he achieved success . . . we've got a little bleeder here, can I have more suction? Now that rheumatic fever has become such a rare disease, mitral stenosis is far less common.'

They had been standing beneath the merciless theatre lights for nearly two hours. Liz began to feel exhausted by the unaccustomed tension and constricted movement. Hugh, though, continued to radiate that supreme confidence and enjoyment in his intricate task. Liz wondered how his back muscles could stand it. No wonder he took pains to keep himself at the peak of fitness and to drive his system to the physical limits. The lives of others depended upon him.

'Shall I finish for you, Hugh?'

'No, thanks, Mother F., I'll see this one off the table. Guess we could all sink a coffee, though, eh?' In went the last few sutures and Sister Cecilia moved in to swab the incision with chlorhexidine. A neat strip of plaster to finish — and all was safely over.

As she drove back to the Casa in the late afternoon, alone, Liz reflected that this had been a most invigorating day. She swung the Mini past the garage and parked well out of Hugh's way. He was still at the Clinic, watching over Anne Leigh Bycroft's post-operative condition. Luisa had left a letter from England on the hall table, addressed to Liz in her mother's neat, cursive hand. She carried it into the kitchen and slit open the envelope with the bread knife, poured an ice-cold *citron pressé*, and read the news from home perched on the poolside, bare toes dabbling in the sparkly blue depths.

Hugh should have been exhausted after a long operating schedule in which the mitral valvotomy was but one of a backlog of heart cases awaiting surgery. Instead, like an actor after a demanding performance, the adrenalin still surged, unquenched even by twenty lengths of the pool in a chilly evening breeze.

'Get your glad rags on, Nurse Larking, I'm taking you out to dinner. We both deserve some relaxation after such a busy day. I've booked a table at the Castelo Laranja.'

'The *Castelo*!' Liz blinked in astonishment. Why, the Castelo was for the likes of Roger Moore or Joan Collins — fearfully grand and expensive. 'What on earth can I wear?' she asked herself in excited consternation. *Dynasty*-style dresses would be the order of the day.

'Wear that white thing — the one I saw you in that night I had to fly back to London . . . '

But even as he spoke, Hugh's active brain was putting two and two together. He'd wondered at the time why Liz was looking such a dream . . . and of course, with hindsight, the reason was crystal clear. She must have left him at Faro and gone on to some club with Richard Bycroft. Then, while the cat was away, that rat must have had the run of the Casa de la Paz.

Yet again Liz was wishing she could read the surgeon's fathomless mind — one moment smiling at her, the very next glaring as if he hated the sight of her. After the stresses of the day, the trauma of watching Anne's operation, the undeniable thrill of seeing for herself that Hugh was one of the greatest heart surgeons in action, Liz couldn't get a grip on herself and she literally began to shake . . . whatever was the matter with Hugh? Didn't he have any conception of what it did to someone if one moment you raised them to the heights of happiness and then, with deliberate cruelty and the most heart-stopping volte-face, plunged from approval to utter contempt?

Whatever — in the space of seconds — could she have done to have given such offence?

'Be ready in an hour,' he said shortly, and turned on his disdainful heel.

Liz showered quickly and shampooed her hair which was sticky from being confined in a theatre cap. To give herself added height she decided to scoop it all up on top of her head in an Edwardian onion, with wispy trails of curls framing her small and wistful face. Tonight was going to test all the confidence she could summon, with Hugh in one of his strange and unpredictable moods. She'd make sure she looked really nice, then forget all about her appearance and concentrate on being — alone — with Hugh. It was, after all, the major theme of all her dreams, waking and sleeping.

So Liz darkened her eyelids with smoky shadows and painted her mouth with cherry gloss. Her one good piece of jewellery was the seed pearl necklet and earrings her godmother had given her for her eighteenth birthday. Against the fine golden skin of her shoulders in the sundress, the tiny delicate pearls gleamed with an iridescence that reflected the brave little fount of excitement that quickened her heart-beat. Last time she'd looked like this and hoped for an evening just like this, it had all gone wrong. But nothing was going to spoil her pleasure tonight. She had no intention of putting a foot wrong.

\* \* \*

'I noticed you looking a bit green when I made the first incision,' remarked Hugh pleasantly over the seafood platter. 'I thought you might be going to crash out on us.'

'Oh, really?' countered Liz with brave sarcasm and another draught of champagne, 'I don't usually go in for green face powder. Are you sure you weren't confused by my emerald eye-shadow? There wasn't much else of me on display.'

'Made up for that now, though, haven't you?' A significant eye explored

Liz's efforts to disguise her cleavage with a full-blown white rose. Things matured early in the Algarve.

Her cheeks went slightly pink. 'That's hardly polite,' she pointed out in a voice that came out rather prim and proper.

'Am I ever polite?' grinned Hugh in that heartrending fashion that turned her bones to water.

'Isn't the food delicious!' she gulped. It was as she feared — out of her depth in a twosome with the sophisticated Hugh Forsythe who was as usual thoroughly enjoying himself baiting his young companion. He dismembered a prawn and held it out to her lips, his fingers dripping with the luscious buttery juices. Deliberately he allowed his fingers to brush with butterfly delicacy against her lips; so deliberately that Liz almost choked with the effort to breathe normally and swallow at one and the same time. She snatched up her glass and hid behind it, her fingers playing with the crystal stem.

'Thirsty,' she mumbled, as those

amused black eyes travelled thoughtfully over her vivid mouth and glittering
eyes.

'Not to worry — I'm the one who's
driving. Drink up — there's plenty
more where this came from.'

Oh yes, thought Liz, you'd love to get
me drunk, wouldn't you? Silly little
idiot, you'd think, who can't hold her
liquor. 'Do they breathalyse people out
here?'

Hugh grimaced. 'I've never put that
to the test. Having done my whack of
patching people up in casualty depart-
ments, if I had my way they'd hang,
draw and quarter drunken drivers.'

Liz blenched. Trust Hugh to have decided
and colourful opinions on every subject
under the sun! Her eyes swivelled to the
other diners, exploring the opulence of
the gilded candlelit dining-room, the glittering scene reflected in the great baroque
mirrors dominating every wall. 'I had
hoped we might dine out on the balcony beneath the stars — I hadn't bargained
on a rising gale. Good thing I latched all

the shutters before we left.'

In the heat of day, wooden shutters could be drawn across the windows to keep the house cool. By night, if the wind got up, they tended to bang against the outside walls and disturb the sleepers within.

The wind had indeed increased to a surprising strength, but its howl was drowned by the string orchestra, playing, mused Liz, music to smooch by, tugging at the heartstrings and making her feet itch to dance to those insidious rhythms. Several couples were already swaying on the raised arena of the intimate dance floor. It was all very luxurious, very discreet, very sensual. And doubtless extremely expensive.

Hugh, the mind-reader, stood up and tugged at the lapels of his cream dinner jacket. 'May I have the pleasure?' he murmured. An elegant, formal bow, belied by the warmth of his regard as Liz rose gracefully to her feet. That earlier black mood had quite disappeared, never, she prayed fervently, to return. At least not for the next few hours! Just as one might have expected, Hugh moved expertly into a tricky foxtrot — was there nothing he did not do with supreme and confident ease? — and for the next five minutes concentrated on matching her inexperienced steps to his.

'With a little more practice, young woman, you'll be a pleasure to dance with. Ah, here are our steaks — delicious!' He refilled her glass with a red Rioja, then raised his own in a toast. 'Here's to some *more* practice,' he said meaningfully. No doubt with Bycroft Liz did that remote-control stuff which put yards between the couple. Good luck to them!

'Foxtrots are a bit tricky, aren't they? Paul taught me the waltz and the quickstep and I'm quite good at those.'

'I like the old-fashioned dances,' said Hugh with relish. 'I like to get a grip on my partner.'

'I bet you do,' laughed Liz with cheeky charm. 'Round the throat!'

Hugh leaned his weight on both arms and lowered those idiosyncratic eyebrows, capturing her gaze with eyes that mesmerised. 'If you carry on like that, *Elizabeth*, I shall have to teach you the error of your ways. When we get back home.'

'Oh dear,' murmured Liz with a smile on her lips and her heart in her eyes, thinking back to the arrogant stranger she had clashed with all those weeks ago on the flight to Faro. Who could have believed she would end up falling in love with such a man?

They finished eating and rose once more to dance, Hugh's chin settling against the side of her forehead, his hand warm and comforting against the bare skin of her back, the white rose in her bodice quite crushed by their intimate closeness, Hugh crooning gently in her delighted ear.

At last Liz tilted back her head and chuckled out loud, interrupting the tuneless growl emerging from the region of Hugh's black silk bow-tie.

'So? You find my singing less than irresistible?' grinned her partner.

You're wholly irresistible, Mr Forsythe! sighed her eyes, but her lips were more circumspect. 'What a relief to discover something you're *not* a master of!'

Hugh's grip intensified to iron and he pulled her even closer, thinking to himself this wasn't very wise, to give himself away like this, but God! it was wonderful. And tonight they would be all alone in the house together. And the way Liz was looking at him . . .

When he released her so suddenly, striding back to their table and looking grimly satisfied about something, Liz was in total confusion. The band was in the middle of *Blue Moon* and she couldn't have been more content there in Hugh's arms, their bodies moving together as one. Yet he had broken away on an abrupt mid-step, expecting her to follow like a meek little lamb, with no explanation for his . . . his *rudeness* . . .

Just then a young man blocked her path as she wove her way between the tables to join Hugh, who was already seated and refilling his glass. 'May I have this dance? I — er — I've been watching you for some time.'

Liz accepted with a slow nod of assent, her eyes darting back to Hugh, her head dipping like a flower on the golden stem of her fragile neck.

'I see you've made another conquest,' he observed as she returned to her own seat, amused to see how much the 'another' startled her. 'Nice for you to be with someone your own age. Did he think I was your father or something?' He indicated for the puddings trolley to be brought over, but Liz shook her head and asked for cheese and biscuits. 'I do happen to know how old you are,' she said coolly. 'And I don't happen to think thirty-four is verging on senility. His name is Felix, he's twenty-two — and his parents are right over there. I found him very relaxing after sparring with you.'

'Don't you mean *boring*?' challenged Hugh with a smile that showed his uneven pointed white teeth. He speared a piece of cheese and held it temptingly out to her. Liz shook her head and hitched up the front of her dress. Felix had held her so clumsily she could still feel the hot sweaty imprint of his palm through the white cotton covering her lower back. She hoped it hadn't made a dirty mark. She looked up and found the surgeon regarding her with a wholly unguarded look of pleasure. Irresistibly she smiled back at him. Whatever Hugh was up to, whatever game he was playing with her — somehow she knew she could trust him, that he would never let her come to any harm.

Inevitably the evening drew to an end and the orchestra tuned in to the last waltz. Liz and Hugh danced without speaking, as though there was no need for words, no longing for anything more than to be in each other's arms. At least that was how it seemed to Liz. When their self-absorption was interrupted she could have cried out aloud in despair as her ecstasy crumbled . . .

Of all misfortune — Rosita and Rodrigo Vedras! 'We just dropped in for a nightcap, darlings. How amusing to find you two here!' Familiarly Rosita reached up and kissed Hugh, her scarlet talons gripping the shoulder of his jacket as though she held him in her power, as seductively poised as a serpent. A serpent with a venomous tongue as she whispered her secrets into Hugh's disdainful ear. Before Liz's eyes his face hardened and his mouth tautened with distaste.

Turning her pleading eyes on the silent Senhor Vedras, Liz was stunned with a further blow. All he could offer was a slight shake of his head and a glance of weary cynicism — as if his wife's machinations had ceased to concern him. Why did Hugh allow it? What poison was Rosita dripping into his ears?

Suddenly Hugh shrugged the woman off. The alcohol on her breath sickened him; if emotional blackmail was Rosita's game then he would not take part. They had done nothing wrong, nor would do so.

'Liz flies home on Tuesday. This is a final thank-you for all her hard work. I fear she hasn't found me the ideal employer.'

Whatever was he saying? Liz went hot, then cold. When had Hugh decided she must leave so soon?

'Is that so?' drawled Rosita with languid insolence. 'Well, don't try too hard to make it up to her, will you? . . . Now do join us for one last drink, Hugh darling. And you too, of course,' she added, her sneering eyes examining Liz just as if she could see the home-turned hem and the churning heart inside that shapely bodice.

'I'm afraid we have to go,' interrupted Hugh shortly. 'I'll call into your office, Rodrigo. We need to talk about maintenance of the grounds and swimming pool.'

'That woman must be drunk,' he

muttered as he steered Liz away. 'I've seen a different side to Rosita this year. I can't think how a decent chap like Rodrigo puts up with her antics.'

Liz was silent all the way back to the Casa de la Paz. She refused to ask just when Hugh had decided to send her packing with such peremptory notice. The grim silhouette of his profile and the aggressive way he swung the big car along narrow roads and braked harshly at every corner told only too clearly of his change of mood. He wanted her out of his life as fast as possible. Out of his thoughts. Out of his home.

When they crunched to a halt on the gravel drive, Liz was out of the car in a flash, the wind tearing at her clothes and her hair as she struggled to the front door, snatched up the key from under the lily pot and let herself in to the Casa de la Paz.

'It's the best thing for both of us!' she told herself fiercely as she flung off her clothes and scrubbed away the last traces of warpaint. 'It would be very embarrassing for you, wouldn't it, Mr Forsythe, to have me trailing round the Hanoverian making sheep's eyes on account of a bit of idle holiday flirtation? Better for both of us if I go home now before you have to deal with my broken heart!'

# 9

During the night the winds flayed themselves into a frenzy. There would be no fish for the markets in the morning. The fishing boats sheltered safe in harbour.

Before he went to sleep, Hugh stepped out on to his balcony to retrieve a sunbed which was thumping with monotonous regularity against the bedroom wall. There was enough on his mind without that extra aggravation. Yet in a peculiar way he identified himself with the night, felt a part of its rage. It was as if a veil had lifted to show him Rosita in her magnificent malevolence. Hell hath no fury . . .

He had spoken on the spur of the moment when he told them Liz was leaving — a rare thing in a man not given to impulsive words or deeds. A man trained, however, to consider all the options at the speed of light; and to act upon his decision, knowing the consequences must be momentous. When Liz went, Hugh knew he might see her again. But in a very different world where she would be among people her own age, with all the excitement and stimulus of a new environment. There would be no chance to pick up where they had left off. Too busy once more for Hugh to adjust his life to include love.

And there was one other imperative reason why Liz must be sent packing. With narrowed eyes Hugh stared out over the seething landscape, unfamiliar now beneath the blanket of the night. Though the air was warm, the gale tore at his hair and his jacket, and he didn't intend to stay outside much longer. Clouds whipped across the face of the moon and blotted out the pinpricks of starlight. It was, he thought bitterly, the wildest night he had experienced at the Casa over all the years.

In the early hours Liz awoke with a

start. Something troubled her — some sound that should not be . . . something not quite right, yet very close to her room.

It came again, that sound.

Liz was instantly wide awake. She sat up in bed, the covers dragged up to her chin, her scalp prickling with fright. The stealthy tread of footsteps, there outside her french window. Had she locked it? She must have! Someone was creeping along the patio — and Hugh so far away in his balcony suite. An ice-cold sweat broke out on her brow. A deliberate hand was on the shutter, testing its luck. Liz stifled a scream and slid from her bed. In the dark it wasn't possible to be sure, but the curtain had moved with the door handle being turned. Thank God Hugh must have checked all the doors before they went out to dine. But he must be warned immediately. The outside staircase led directly up to his balcony. Anyone could walk in while he slept!

In the blackness Liz somehow laid

hand on her stripey shirt and with fumbling, agonised fingers struggled with the buttons. On bare feet she fled along the passage towards the stairs and Hugh. But as she passed the front door more sounds froze her into a terrified statue. Someone was attacking the heavy front door, scraping away at the lock of the stout carved wood . . . Liz galvanised her appalled body into action and burst up the stairs and into Hugh's bedroom without so much as by your leave.

'What the hell . . . ' snapped Hugh, instantly alert from years of coping with the emergencies of the night.

'B-b burglars!' hissed Liz between chattering teeth. 'Trying to break in downstairs. Come quickly, Hugh — they're sawing at the lock on the front door!'

Hugh flung aside the bedclothes and Liz quickly averted her eyes. If her employer chose not to bother with pyjamas then that was none of her business. 'You stay here,' he ordered, seizing a pair of shorts, his dark silhouette reassuringly massive in the grainy half-light. Liz almost felt sorry for the intruders. If he got his hands on them . . .

'You're not leaving me on my own,' she gasped. 'Anyway, shouldn't we be whispering?'

'Whatever for?' snapped back the surgeon, throwing on the lights as he stormed across the landing, filling the house with the stamp of his heavy footsteps and the boom of his deep baritone voice. He thundered down to the front door, unbolted and threw it wide. He strode out into the garden and circled the entire building with Liz cowering in his wake. Up at the farm, the dogs were barking their heads off, disturbed by strange events in the night.

'I didn't imagine things, I swear it,' insisted Liz firmly, annoyed with herself for being so terrified earlier on. Hugh would think she was one of those girls who screamed at the sight of a mouse.

'Indeed you did not,' came the grim

response. 'Take a look at this.' He shone his torchlight on to the flowerbeds and there around the walls of the Casa Liz could clearly see the sandy soil churned and imprinted by the pattern of training shoes. They examined the gouges on the heavy front door. 'Done with a chisel, I'd say. Not a very serious effort considering the weight of this door and the thickness of the wood. If we hadn't disturbed them, they'd have still been here at breakfast trying to prise the lock out.' He switched his examination to the solemn white face staring trustingly up at him. 'Cheer up! Just youngsters, I expect, come out from one of the inland cities and looking for cash or cameras, that sort of thing. They probably thought the noise of the wind was good enough cover.'

Reaction had left Liz exhausted and shivering. 'Please, Hugh — may I sleep on your floor for the rest of the night? My room is so far away from you.'

That scarred eyebrow quirked in wry amusement. 'What you need is a strong hot cup of tea. This isn't the Liz I remember, fearless and full of guts.'

The state of my guts, thought Liz wretchedly as she followed him into the kitchen, is decidedly queasy. It's all right for a great tough guy like Hugh Forsythe to know he can dominate any situation. Five foot two, and half his weight . . . what's a girl supposed to do when danger threatens?

And what, jeered her conscience, makes you think his bedroom is safer than your own? Just look at him!

What do you think I'm doing? scowled Liz. Sitting here while *he* makes *me* a soothing cuppa! His hair all tousled, just wearing white shorts, brown bare hunk of a man.

She drooped against the cupboards, her feet pinched and blue with cold, her thoughts as steamy as the mug of tea Hugh pushed into her trembling hands. Sure enough, the hot sweet drink revived her courage and stilled the shivers. Her own bed once more seemed inviting . . .

Hugh ran his eyes over her from head to foot, shook his head and moved to stand directly in front of the tired girl. Liz made no protest when he placed a hand on either side of her rib-cage and lifted and set her on the working top, then chafed her small blue toes with warm vigorous fingers. But when those same fingers reached deliberately for the buttons of her shirt Liz's reaction was automatic. 'No!' Her hands closed over her buttons with grim determination to save the situation from what seemed inevitable.

'No!' Avoiding his eyes, she turned her head aside. Their consciences must remain clear. Hugh was still married, she felt certain of it. However lonely he might be, stuck out there with only a naïve little nurse for company, he should have no cause for regrets, for that much he would remember her and be grateful . . .

'What are you doing?' At the sight of those determined little white knuckles, Hugh gave a roar of laughter. A hand clamped down on her head and Liz was forced to see for herself, the humiliation welling up in a choking torrent. 'I was just trying to tidy you up, you dishevelled little creature, since you don't appear to have learned how to dress yourself! There — does that put your suspicious mind at rest?'

Mortified, Liz sorted out her buttons for herself. Her sole concern had been for Hugh, his safety, the beast. 'I don't need your help,' she retorted huffily as he towered over her, hands on his hips, looking typically pleased with himself in that darkly saturnine way.

'Can't have you getting into bed with chilly little toes,' said Hugh in that blandly annoying manner, well calculated to get her back up. In spite of her protests he gathered Liz up in his arms, strode across the kitchen and out into the hall, ignoring her struggles with infuriating purposefulness. Knowing full well that this was not the way to her bedroom, he set off up the stairs and without bothering to switch on the lights dumped her none too gently on to his wide double bed.

All the fight went out of Liz. The sheets were still warm from his body. If it really was what he wanted, then why not admit her defences were down; give in, submit? A girl could only try so hard . . .

Of their own accord her arms stretched up to Hugh, clasped at the back of his neck and pulled him down to her as he leaned over the bed. With ardent fierceness their lips met and clung and he lowered his body down on to hers . . . Then shock replaced joy as Liz found herself rejected, pushed harshly back against the pillows as with an oath Hugh swung himself off the bed and stepped back and away from her, his voice hard and cold. 'Since neither of us seems very responsible tonight you'd better stay here and I'll take your bed. We're safer far apart — burglars or no burglars.'

Liz lay rigid with shame and misery. It had been her fault, in spite of her intentions. If she had not made the first move, they would never . . . he could never . . .

In the doorway Hugh paused and looked back at her. She imagined the look in his eyes, for it was too dark to tell the expression on his face, the mingled regret and desire for what might have been. For one heart-stopping moment Liz imagined he would change his mind and come back to her. 'Tell Luisa to get those sheets changed, Liz,' he remarked matter-of-factly. 'Your feet are absolutely filthy running about like that outside! Sleep tight.'

And by the time Liz had summoned up strength to hurl a pillow at the door, he was gone.

★   ★   ★

Hugh was up early next morning, checking the villa by daylight and going up to the farm to see if Luisa's sister had heard anything in the night. He was

278

keen to be off, to make an examination of Anne Leigh Bycroft's post-operative condition. When Liz came creeping down to breakfast she found he had almost finished eating the ham she had got in for supper, and the eggs had been polished off as well.

'You look like death warmed up!'

Liz curled her lip and glared from under heavy eyelids. Trust Hugh Forsythe to state the obvious! She swallowed a couple of pills and gulped down some black coffee. Through the kitchen window a light drizzle began to darken the ochre soil — not sufficient, observed Hugh, to be much comfort to the farmers; but the countryside would take on a new life. He suggested a picnic for the following day so Liz could admire the fresh burst of blossom and get a closer look at the Monchique hills with their famous drinking waters and fantastic views. 'A good way to see the flora and fauna — '

' — and say goodbye to the Algarve,' Liz finished for him with a dry edge to her words, remembering how she had received the news of her imminent departure. He might have had the decency to tell her direct rather than inform the world at large that she was going. If the Monchique trip was a salve to his conscience then she refused to grovel with gratitude; after all, she had a car at her disposal, could go where she liked. She did not need him as her escort.

'We can say goodbye to the Algarve together,' Hugh observed surprisingly gently, as though aware of her unhappiness.

Liz glanced up in surprise. 'Are you leaving too? But I thought — ?'

He shook his head. 'Not on your flight.' They stared at each other, so many things left unsaid. Then, 'I see,' said Liz flatly. She ran hot water into the sink, added washing up liquid and started on the dishes. 'I should like to say goodbye to Anne if I may. Would that be possible?'

'Come this afternoon, then. Your smiling face will cheer her up.'

Liz grimaced at his departing back. Sarcastic as ever! He might guess, if he only took the trouble, how miserable she must be feeling.

What was Mother going to make of it when Liz suddenly appeared back home and said the job was over? They'd been expecting her to stay till the end of June, when Hugh himself would have returned to the Hanoverian.

Liz shivered. After last night's events she wasn't sure she fancied staying as caretaker at the Casa, alone and with not another soul within earshot. At heart she was a coward, she realised with a rueful sigh. And without Hugh? Ah, how could she have anticipated the way he would take over her life and all its hopes and dreams? If he was going back to London too, then she might just as well resign herself to the inevitable and go home to Mother.

If it was to be done at all, then it must be done now, with Hugh tied up at the Clinic for the whole of the day. Oh, Liz knew she'd had the chance several times within the past few days. But flesh and spirit had refused to act, and she had just shied away from discovery like an ostrich that prefers to bury its head in the sand rather than face reality.

Luisa was being infuriatingly slow this morning, working at a snail's pace as she dusted and mopped and swept. It was twelve before Liz heard her call goodbye, and she had only an hour left before she too must drive over to the Clinic to see Anne. One hour, though, should be enough to invade Hugh's privacy, to go through his belongings like a thief, intrude upon his pain and probe his memories.

Supposing he'd locked his study door? Her hand already upon the brass knob, Liz felt sick. But Hugh was trusting and barred no one entry.

She stood there in the centre of the room, her unhappy eyes ranging over shelves crammed with books, the typewriter with its dust cover in place. The desk, with a table drawn up beside it to take the overflow of his research papers in their copious piles. No photographs, no pictures, not one snapshot to testify to the reality of his marriage.

In the event, it didn't take Liz long to find the leather-bound album with its silken tassel, there in the bottom drawer of Hugh's desk where he could reach with ease to mull bitterly upon a tragic past.

Her hands were numb as she crossed unsteadily to the window and found herself examining a fledgling Casa de la Paz, the garden newly planted, the swimming pool a muddy chasm, presided over by two grinning workmen and a churning cement mixer.

Penelope smiled back at her from every page.

Liz had found it impossible to visualise a woman to match up to Hugh Forsythe. But here was the one. What a ghastly loss!

Trembling from head to foot Liz shoved the album of photos back where she had found it and raced from the study to the kitchen, where she made herself swallow a strong, hot cup of coffee, burning her mouth yet heedless of the pain. *It wasn't Penelope in Room Ten*. The colouring, the exquisite bone structure, those enchanting slant-set eyes. Poor Hugh.

Who then was the woman he agonised over in Room Ten?

★   ★   ★

Liz jumped into the Mini and dashed off to the shops in Praia da Oura, loading up with enough provisions to see them through the weekend, cold meats and fruits and cheeses for the promised picnic. They were expecting her at the Clinic — her last visit to Anne, her farewells to all the staff and the patients.

She drove fast, much too fast. But she was going to find out just who was in Room Ten, and set her heart at rest. The knowledge that Hugh was free to marry had set up a foolish, irrational surge of elation. The gulf between their stations in life loomed as unbridgeable as ever it had. And he wanted her out of his life. Those were the hard facts. But Liz knew her love for him dissolved them to superable proportions. Back in London. You never knew. It wasn't such a hopeless dream . . . was it?

Luck was on Liz's side. Sister Cecilia was in Room Ten seeing to her patient's comfort, chatting softly to the poor woman as if she could hear and comprehend every reassuring word. Liz lent a willing hand, then drew the nun over to the window. 'Sister! It's so hard to say goodbye to you all . . . and I don't suppose I'll ever be able to get back, even to visit you — '

That wonderfully calm face smiled and smiled. There was a suspicion, Liz realised with some perplexity, of a twinkle in the Sister's eyes. People didn't usually look so pleased at the prospect of parting for ever. 'No?' responded the nun — just as if she knew something Liz should have done but was too blind to recognise. 'Well, we shall just have to see.'

Liz nodded helplessly in polite agreement. No one, surely, could read the future, even a professed and saintly nun. But if she ever got the smallest chance — yes, she would return.

'The Little Flower — if ever I do come back, will she still be lying here suspended between life and death?' Liz was speaking half to herself, half aloud, her compassionate gaze focused on the woman in the bed.

'They'll reach a decision soon. Mother Flora needs this bed, but that's of no consequence at all. It's the quality of life that concerns us here and now. When Mr Forsythe can come to terms with his conscience, then the ventilator can be switched off and this poor dear lady kept from her Maker no longer.' It was clear from the way she spoke that Sister felt the decision had been over-long postponed. A chill finger traced the channel of Liz's spine.

'Mr Forsythe's conscience — but I don't understand. Is the patient a relative of his?'

Sister Cecilia peered at the bed consideringly. Yes, she supposed it was possible to mistake the Senhora for a Briton. 'No, no, of course she isn't. This is a local lady who came to the Clinic for help — one of our charitable patients to whom we offer treatment without charge. It was nothing of great significance, a straightforward operation. There was no blame to be attached to any member of the surgical team. What's saddest of all is that no one bothers to visit her now, and the husband, as I hear, will marry again as soon as our Little Flower dies.'

'But what *happened*?' Demanded Liz in an anguished whisper. 'Mr Forsythe clearly blames himself for *something*.'

'One hour after the operation she collapsed with a heart attack and suffered severe and permanent brain damage. Hugh Forsythe's only error has been to let himself become over-emotionally involved with this patient's situation. His own wife had just died. He had to come to terms with the knowledge that in spite of all his skills, he was helpless. Now the husband no longer even visits, and the two young children are brought up by another woman and allowed to forget their real mother.'

'How dreadful!' Liz felt sick. How many times had she heard Paul say no doctor could afford to empathise with his patients — not if he were to hang on to his sanity.

'He's one in a million,' observed the nun shrewdly as conflicting emotions flickered across the expressive young face. 'After Penelope's death we were all very anxious for Hugh. It's a very vulnerable time. But he's a strong character with a definite philosophy to guide him. Perhaps as members of a religious community we reach our conclusions by another path; but our aim and our purpose is to heal and comfort. And though hearts can be made to beat and lungs to breathe long after a person has lost consciousness for ever, Hugh is coming to the same conclusion, that preserving life at all costs is not the answer.'

In Anne's room, there lay the evidence of the sheer happiness Hugh's great skills could bring. Gone the mitral stenosis and the struggle to breathe, and in its place a radiant Anne who felt stronger than she could ever remember. It was nothing short of a miracle, she declared: without doubt she would be working again this summer. Every other sentence emphasised her gratitude to Hugh — and to Liz for the part she had played in overcoming Anne's reluctance to seek medical help.

Out in the car park Liz was just about to climb back into the Mini when a voice hailed her and she turned to see Richard Bycroft, half obscured behind an enormous bouquet for his mother.

'Wow! A walking flower stall!'

'Just the girl I most wanted to see! You and I have something to celebrate,

Liz Larking. Dine with me tonight, *se faz favor*. Be my guest at the Hotel Vicente and we'll dance the night away.' Flashing his strong white teeth in that boyish grin, Richard delved into his bouquet and extracted one perfect rose which he handed to Liz with a flourish. In his elegantly tailored suit of turquoise linen his stunning good looks were set off to perfection. The sunshine filled his golden curls with light so that they framed his head like an angel's halo. Against her better judgment Liz found herself quite dazzled. Yes, Richard would be amusing and distracting company. An evening with him would be better spent than moping about the Casa in anticipation of parting from Hugh. '*Muy obrigada!*' she smiled, lifting the pink flower to her nostrils and breathing in its rich perfume. 'I haven't had the chance to thank you for the rose you sent me . . . '

'Then thank me tonight, if you must. I've been *longing* to see you again.'

Liz laughed out loud. 'Flatterer!' she

teased, and Richard joined in with a grin of engaging candour. Liz was a refreshing change from his usual type of giddy girl-friend.

'I've just left your mother. She's feeling like a million dollars — '

'And you're looking it!' came back the charming, instant response.

Liz glanced down at her bare legs and short denim skirt. What it was, she mused, still smiling to herself as she unlocked the driver's door and settled herself behind the wheel, to have been gifted with a golden tongue to match that fabulous face and body. But she still wasn't sure what to make of Richard Bycroft; he was totally unlike any man she'd ever known before. It was a bit disconcerting, such deliberate double-cream *charm*. Though Liz knew she couldn't trust Richard one inch where affairs of the heart were concerned, at least he made it perfectly clear he was out for sexual conquest. Whereas Hugh was a mystery, unfathomable. What went on behind those inscrutable black eyes was anybody's guess. Not that it mattered now, when it was far from likely their lives would conflict ever again . . .

Neither she nor Richard had noticed the tall white-coated figure who paused in the corridor and stared out at them from a discreet window, his face grave with an unfathomable expression.

When she made her announcement that evening that Hugh's supper was prepared and in the oven, but that she would be dining out with Mrs Leigh Bycroft's son, Liz was slightly disappointed that not a flicker of emotion crossed her employer's impassive face. And yet she knew he must disapprove . . . The implacable control of the surgeon! she decided. Not an inkling of emotion to betray to her that he was not after all impervious. It made her behaviour last night even more reprehensible.

Liz bit her lip, helplessly enthralled by recollection. Had she just imagined the electricity of that kiss? Surely not. It took two to generate such thrilling excitement. Yet here she stood, about to walk away from him and into the embrace of a golden younger man, and Hugh quite clearly did not give a fig.

'Enjoy yourself. I shan't wait up.' His eyes coursed over her bare shoulders, that white dress, the high-heeled sandals that set off her small feet and slim ankles. Liz had pressed the cotton with care to freshen it, fastened the pink rose in the low neckline, dressed her hair so that it swept seductively behind one ear, held by a comb, curled in a mass of soft waves over her shoulders. 'You look very nice,' said Hugh heavily. 'Want a drink before you go?'

'Thank you — but no. There, I can hear Richard now.' In answer Hugh swung on his heel and strode off to his study, leaving Liz with the image lingering long after in her mind of his laconic figure retreating from her, hands stuffed into the pockets of narrow dark slacks, his white shirt clinging to the outlines of his strongly muscled back. She sighed and went to answer the doorbell.

The Hotel Vicente took her quite by surprise. Liz made no attempt to conceal her delight by a pretence of weary sophistication, as some girls might have on finding themselves in such a charmingly distinguished atmosphere. It was rather like being a guest in the country home of some wealthy Portuguese nobleman, surrounded by his family portraits and heirlooms. No wonder Anne loved coming here! 'I feel as if I'm in the home of some patrician family who've fallen on hard times and been obliged to take in paying guests!' she said delightedly.

'Exactly how we planned it,' approved Richard with evident satisfaction. 'I'm delighted you find it so.' He poured chilled white wine into elegant crystal glasses and sat down beside Liz, his arm instantly settling about her. You certainly don't waste time, do you? thought Liz, and decided her best policy was to be equally straightforward. She lifted off his hand, set it back on his own knee, patted it nicely and said, 'There, that's better.'

Richard flung back his head and chortled, revealing those splendid teeth of his. 'You can't blame a guy for trying, Liz. Not when you're so darned attractive.'

'I've never seen a hotel so filled with beautiful people. I must be the most ordinary girl here.'

'But I'm bored with all of them, Liz. What's so refreshing about you is you say and do what you think — you don't put on some act pretending to have done it all, seen everything. And I find you a quite irresistible challenge, the way you won't just fall into my arms.'

Liz sat up straight. 'Yes, I thought that might be it. Do you know, I'm incredibly starved? I could eat the proverbial horse!'

Richard got up and pressed a bell in the wall. 'Thank heaven for a girl who isn't on a diet. My private dining room is just through there. All will be ready for us in five minutes.'

Liz bit her lip. She would have felt safer in a crowd with Richard Bycroft. Still, doubtless there would be a waiter or two hovering around to serve the manager and his personal guest. And perhaps later they could join in the dancing downstairs in the ballroom. An experiment to test her reactions in another man's arms . . .

Two laden trolleys had been wheeled into the dining-room and plugged into wall sockets to keep the food warm. It was dark outside now and the lamps cast a soft rosy light on the round table with its white damask cloth and centrepiece of flowers. A rich savoury aroma hung on the air and Liz, relaxed in spite of finding herself quite alone with Richard, sniffed with hungry relish. For all her qualms he was not obviously bent on seduction; her drinks had been just sufficient to sharpen her appetite rather than turn her head.

For such a heartbreaking charmer he

proved an affable and considerate companion. Well, Liz chided herself, what else might one expect, seeing his mother was Anne Leigh Bycroft? One delectable course followed another. 'I am making a pig of myself, aren't I?'

Richard raised his glass to her. 'I take that as a compliment. More wine, madame?'

Placing her knife and fork neatly together, Liz leaned back in her chair and sighed with deep satisfaction. This was much more pleasant than an evening of gloom back at the Casa. 'May I ask you an impertinent question, Richard?'

He shrugged expansively. 'Ask away.'

'Well, what puzzles me is this. Why are you running a hotel — superior establishment though it clearly is — when I should have thought with your contacts you could be making a fortune in the theatre — or in films? I mean to say,' she continued recklessly, 'you're quite extraordinarily good-looking, aren't you . . .'

An eloquent hand clutched at his

forehead in a dramatic gesture. 'Liz! I feared you'd never notice . . . seriously though, I must confess to early ambitions along those lines. After all, it was a world I grew up in, was familiar with. But the answer's quite simple. Fate decided otherwise.' Carefully he lifted the bottle from the ice bucket and refilled her glass without spilling a drop.

'Yes?' Liz urged him on, her eyes wide above the rim of her glass, expectant of some disastrous revelation that would shock her into pity for him. Six months to live perhaps, a sentence of death hanging over him?

'It's ironic really,' continued Richard in sepulchral tones, gazing sadly into her sympathetic eyes. 'I mean — yes, I do look in the mirror and see something special reflected back at me. And you're right — girls almost literally throw themselves at me. But I was not meant to be — ' he paused, 'a sex symbol.'

'Go on, go on. What happened?'

Richard raised his eyes to the ceiling.

'Well, dear, you see I've got this sensitive skin and I'm allergic to *all* forms of theatrical make-up. So there you are!'

'Seriously?' breathed Liz. 'One would have expected in this day and age . . . still, it's a good thing you can speak of your tragedy so cheerfully.' The corners of her mouth twitched; she could not help it. 'Some might call it a grave misfortune.'

'Not really,' said Richard blithely. 'I'm a lousy actor anyway — not a splinter of talent has chipped off the old block. I tried my chances at boarding school, and truly the only part you might have described as tailor-made for me was Pinocchio.'

There was a moment's silence as they looked at each other, then the room's high ceiling echoed with the simultaneous burst of their laughter. 'Idiot!' spluttered Liz, 'you really had me fooled for a moment, thinking I was being presented with some dire tragedy. Are you *sure* you're so lacking in talent?'

'Oh, sure I'm sure. And it's true about the sensitive skin too. But there — ' Richard gestured expansively with a wide sweep of his arms, 'who's complaining? Not me. I get to spend most of the year in this beautiful country. And I believe I do my job superbly well. I adore women — and I've a continuous supply of gorgeous girl-friends. What more could a feller want?' He leaned back in his chair and gave Liz a boldly challenging stare.

She returned the challenge with an easy grin. 'We-ell, not *me* for starters . . . '

'Ah, so there *is* someone else!' came the slyly teasing response. 'I knew it, I can always tell. Some guy you've left back home? Or someone you've met out here?'

Liz was obliged to improvise fast. A hot blush had started somewhere round her throat, and she could feel her pulses begin to pound. For comfort Richard was probing far too close.

'What I'd be interested to know,'

probed Richard with a gleam in his eyes, 'is whether Rosita Vedras ever made it with your illustrious Hugh Forsythe. After his wife died she was round at the Casa every five minutes offering this, that and the other. Penny's best friend!'

'Was she?' echoed Liz faintly, thrown into confusion by the implications of Richard's question. 'D-did you know Penny too?' She rubbed at her forehead with indignant fingers. Richard certainly had a cheek if he thought she was going to gossip about the man who had saved his mother's life!

'I haven't been out here long enough,' said Richard, offering an ebony box of cigarettes which Liz instantly refused. 'But Rosita and I had a bit of a thing going last year and she made no bones about her fascination with Forsythe. I was a bit miffed, actually. I mean, you don't discuss that sort of thing with your lover, do you? It's hardly complimentary, I mean to say!'

'How *awful!*' exclaimed Liz with a shiver. She wasn't thinking of Rosita's passion for Hugh — that was hardly fresh news. But for Richard to sit there so casually and talk about having had an affair with a woman they both knew to be married — well, it just seemed so sordid and . . . Liz shook her head in irritation . . . unpleasant. 'Oh, please let's talk about something else,' she said hurriedly, and began asking questions about the history of the hotel buildings and the sort of problems Richard must come up against in his running of the Vicente.

★   ★   ★

In the early hours of the morning Richard's sports car was parked in the drive of the Casa de la Paz. 'Well, Liz, I don't suppose I shall see you again.' Richard sounded genuinely regretful.

'I suppose not,' she replied a trifle heartlessly. 'I'm not likely ever to pass this way again. Perhaps I shall get to see

Anne in England. I'm hoping so.' In the moonlight her face was pale and a little tired, and Richard turned in his seat and looked closely at her. He leaned towards her and paused, waiting to see if she would flinch away from him, then pulled her firmly into his arms.

Liz knew she was experiencing a kiss that was as near professional as you could get. That embrace had been perfectly calculated to set a girl's pulses racing for more. And Richard was not putting on an act; he clearly found her extremely desirable.

She decided she must be the most abnormal creature. Here was a Greek god of an Englishman, right age, unattached, and much more fun to be with than she had expected. Yet his kisses were as meaningless as any other young man's. The touch of his skilful hands raised no sensation whatsoever — other than the desire to get to her own bed and dream once more of the impossible . . .

'I must go,' she insisted gently.

'Thank you for what turned out to be a marvellous evening. It's been fun.'

Slowly Richard released her, started the engine while she smiled at him from the doorstep, waving a last goodbye. Then, supposing the door to be prudently locked, she rummaged under the lily pot for the key.

Oh, Hugh! To have gone to bed and left Casa de la Paz open and unprotected.

Liz shivered, thinking of him alone in the darkened house and at the mercy of intruders. She wondered if he had remembered to speak to that poor Senhor Vedras — to have a wife who carried on so must be an unbearable humiliation! — about protecting the place.

Noiselessly moving through the hall, Liz checked every lock and bolt on the ground floor, and every window fastening, never switching on a light till she was in the privacy of her own room. Hugh Forsythe should not have his sleep interrupted *this* night.

# 10

Liz had the strangest feeling Hugh was about to cancel the picnic. After all, his time was precious — which gave him the perfect excuse to avoid her company.

All through breakfast she watched him out of the corner of an uncertain eye — monosyllabic, crunching his way through four slices of toast like an automaton fuelling its system, uncompromising head concentrated on the sheaf of papers spread before him on the table.

Her hands shook as she passed him his refilled coffee cup; not to worry — he'd never notice. A grunt was all her thanks.

But late morning Hugh strode out of the study and announced that they were off. 'I want this stuff properly typed,' he said tersely. 'We can drop it into the Clinic on our way back tonight.' He shoved the wad of papers into his briefcase and glanced down at Liz, who was nervously twisting a heavy curl round her index finger. 'You ready, then?'

'Will I be okay in espadrilles?' she ventured, 'or ought I to have worn proper boots?' It was, she bit her lip, a daft sort of question, seeing she had no walking shoes with her, nor the slightest clue where to get hold of a pair.

'We're not tackling the Himalayas,' came the sarcastic response. 'You can forget the backpack and crampons.' Seeing her bridle visibly and square that stubborn little chin at him, Hugh just grinned wolfishly. Never happier, scowled Liz, than when he was putting you at your ill-at-ease!

In honour of the occasion Hugh hadn't bothered to shave, and a bluish gleam of beard was clearly visible beneath the tanned and healthy skin. The faded black tee-shirt and the elderly khaki shorts, tanned bare feet thrust into a grubby pair of training shoes. He had the most magnificent legs ... towering there over Liz, his granite eyes travelling over her neatly pressed white shorts and crisp gingham shirt, blue wool sweater looped casually across her shoulders. She traipsed meekly after him as he swung about on his heel and strode to unlock and load the boot of the Renault.

'Why not bring the kitchen sink while you're about it?'

'Good idea,' said Liz sweetly, 'perhaps you'd wrench it off the wall for me.' A most unchivalrous hand caught her a slap on her unguarded rear as she leaned into the boot, stacking things with care against spillages.

'Don't make this trip on my account!' she protested hotly, cracking her head as she jerked up sharply. 'Ouch!' But Hugh had gone back to find his large-scale map of the area they were visiting and the momentary defiance was witnessed by a lone, curious lizard basking on the hot gravel near Liz's feet.

The first ten minutes passed in a silence that had Liz wriggling with discomfort. At length she could bear it no longer. 'Did you speak to Senhor Vedras about security at the house?' she demanded. 'You said you were going to.'

'*Relax!*' There was a moment's pause. 'Just enjoy yourself. Leave the worrying to me.'

Concern overruled Liz's judgment. 'How can I?' she argued in vexed tones, 'knowing you'll be there on your own with no one near enough to hear anything!' Even to her own ears, her voice sounded all shrill with tension.

Hugh took his eyes from the road and glanced briefly at the small, cross person sitting beside him. 'I do appreciate your concern,' he assured her mildly, 'but you're out here as cook, not bodyguard. Now, to change the subject I suggest you concentrate on the scenery. It alters quite remarkably as we get right up into the hills.'

Before long they found themselves

travelling through thickly forested regions along a road dappled with patches of sunlight and shade and winding its way up towards the infertile scalp of the hills. Out of the blue Hugh pulled into a wayside verge and with an exclamation peered back over his shoulder.

'Good lord! I never expected to find this place again. We must have lunch here.'

Liz stared at the little café, its bamboo roof dripping with a rampant blue wisteria. 'But . . . what about the picnic?'

'We'll save that for tea. Come on, out you get. You can't go back to England without sampling chicken *piri-piri*.'

They sat in the open at a wooden trestle table, munching black olives and drinking beer, looking out over the mountain side to the valley below, the scent of wisteria enveloping and heady. When it came, with fresh-baked rolls and salad, the chicken was magnificent and spicy. They ate with their fingers and Liz was amazed to find she had such an appetite. This simple fare was just as tasty as her exotic meal shared with Richard. 'Do you know,' she proclaimed, eyes sparkling and fine tendrils of hair escaping from the confines of her pony-tail, 'I thought dinner at the Vicente was a feast for the gods. But this must be Mount Olympus, and here we are in Zeus's favourite spot eating his favourite food!'

It was a picturesque idea, but Hugh seemed little amused. He picked up a paper napkin and wiped away the juices trickling down her chin before they could fall on to her checked shirt. 'You look like a twelve-year-old,' he chided. But the unspoken reproof hung heavily between them: I don't want to hear about last night, *thank* you very much, Elizabeth.

They drove on until they came to a sleepy village, deserted for the siesta, one sandy mongrel flopped in a patch of shade, tongue out, panting heavily.

'A siesta,' remarked Hugh, 'is just

what I could do with after all that food.'
He set a smart pace, leaving the car and
heading out of the village, clearly
knowing where he was going as he
strode along a meandering path rising
gently through vistas of wild lavender
and mauve and white cistus, greeny
hummocks of sweet-smelling herbs, the
bright orange soil punctuated by grey
boulders and tiny gnarled trees straight
out of a fairy-tale book. This profusion
stretched without end as far as the eye
could see.

'We'll rest here.' Hugh settled himself
in the shade and pulled a Tom Wolfe
paperback from his pocket. Liz was
perfectly happy just to sit and look
about her, watching swallow-tailed
butterflies pirouette from blossom to
blossom.

Suddenly Hugh looked up from his
tale of astronauts and regarded her with
that lopsided ironic smile which never
failed to turn Liz's heart over. How
could he possibly concentrate on
printed words, alone there in such a

romantic spot with a delectable creature like Liz? He sighed heavily. There had been a purpose to this picnic; something weighed heavily on his mind and he had believed that away from the Clinic and the confines of the Casa de la Paz . . . well, it might be easier to see everything in the right perspective. To come to a decision.

Mother Flora had made hers. It wasn't just that they needed the bed — heaven forbid. She would be the last person to let such a thing sway her judgment. No, it was a question of ethics, one of those dilemmas the medical profession had to face in the course of everyday work.

The question in Liz's gentle grey eyes stirred a tenderness in Hugh that made him observe aloud that she possessed the rare gift of stillness and tranquillity. 'I've been watching you — perched there like a little bronze statue, scarcely even blinking. Penny for your thoughts.'

Liz felt her lips tremble and part on a catch of breath. Oh, to be able to open up her heart to Hugh Forsythe! 'I was thinking of Richard,' she lied blatantly, the dishonesty bringing a surge of colour to her face.

'Ah . . . yes.' Hugh's voice was weary with disillusion. He turned his head away from the sight of her. He might have guessed that had happened — heavy physical involvement with the virile young Bycroft. Even the sophisticated Rosita had made a fool of herself where that young man was concerned.

Liz could contain herself not a moment longer. 'I know what you're thinking. But you've got it all wrong, Hugh — please believe me!' A moment ago she had wanted to put him off the trail that led to her own vulnerable heart. Seconds later it hit her with all the subtlety of a sledgehammer that she just couldn't bear the deliberate deceit. If he guessed . . . why then, he guessed. What was the use of pretending, when so soon she'd be gone and could escape the humiliation of Hugh knowing the wretched truth about silly little Liz Larking.

'Just because Richard looks like Lord Byron and Adonis rolled into one — ' Hugh couldn't conceal a smirk of wry amusement at what this conjured up in his mind's eye; Liz sure had a nice line in description! ' — you jump to the conclusion that I must be *infatuated*!' Those heavy black brows were scowling at her now, but Liz was in this right up to her neck and she heedlessly plunged on. 'I dare say *men* find beautiful women irresistible. But let me tell you, Mr Forsythe, a woman seeks something far more interesting and satisfying in her man than superficial good looks.'

Hugh grimaced. A pretty speech indeed. 'I thought you and he seemed more than a little interested in each other in the early hours of this morning.'

Liz sprang to her feet, aghast. 'You were spying on me!'

Hugh curled his lip at the very idea. 'I happened to be enjoying a stroll in the privacy of my own garden. I trust I don't need your permission for that?' He set aside his book and leaned back against the tree, regarding her with narrowed, speculative eyes. He drew the subject back to Richard Bycroft with relentless purpose. 'I'm not suggesting there was any X-certificate stuff — but you weren't fighting the guy off, were you, dear Liz?'

Anger rose like burning lava within her heaving breast. Why did he have to stare at her in that blatant way, his head tilted in that ironical angle of studied amusement? It was dangerous to challenge Hugh Forsythe — you never got quite what you bargained for! 'I'm surprised,' gritted Liz with an attempt at matching his cool, 'that one good night peck should so shock your sense of morality!'

Hugh looked grim now, the planes of his face taut and forbidding. A lump rose in Liz's throat at the intense attractiveness of the man and the depth of her feelings for him.

'I am responsible for your welfare

while you remain under my roof. And I take my responsibilities very seriously.'

Oh, my dear! agonised Liz silently, thinking of Hugh and the terrible decision he must face over his patient at the Clinic. But she hardened her heart to continue this battle of wills. He must hear her out at all costs. She wouldn't leave without making it clear she went under protest. Above all, she didn't want to be thought of as one of Hugh's Forsythe's responsibilities. He had more than enough of those. No! She, Liz, was an independent-minded, able-bodied and professional young woman, one hundred per cent capable of ordering her own life and her relationships.

'Rubbish!' she retorted bitterly. 'Can't you just for once cut off from the 'I'm in charge' bit? Take a proper look and see me as a whole person ... ' *who loves you!* she added with her eyes while a sinister hand squeezed painfully about her lungs.

A faintness came over her, and she

plumped down again, feeling the rough stone of her boulder seat graze the backs of her thighs.

Cold and sarcastic came the measured response. 'Whether you like it or not, Miss Larking, you are going home for your own protection. I intend to put half Europe and the Channel between you and Bycroft — before you come to any serious emotional harm.'

'There's nothing wrong with *my* emotions,' retorted Liz. 'My emotions are perfectly normal. I wouldn't say the same for yours!' As the surgeon's eyebrows reached incredulous heights, she hurried on regardless, 'and it isn't Richard I need protection from — it's you.' Her arms looped defensively about her knees, drawn up as a barrier between the two of them. The utter gall! To admit without the smallest trace of apology that he was sending her home like some giddy adolescent. *For her own good!*

Liz raised both hands in agitation to her hair, seeking relief from the hot and heavy mass of waves pressing down on her heated skull. Hugh sat silently watching her, waiting for her to get it all out of her churning system. 'You must have been blind if you really were out in the garden. Blind not to notice Richard's famous *technique* wasn't having much effect . . .

'You're sending me away for nothing. I couldn't care less if I never see Richard again. But it breaks my heart to think that I — '

'Too late now,' interrupted Hugh, rising to his feet with an air of finality. 'The flight's booked and everything's organised. Besides, I'm due back in London myself for a three-week schedule. You won't be needed here.' He hooked his thumbs in the belt loops of his shorts and looked down on Liz, defiantly standing there right in his path.

'Then bring me back with you!' Hope blazed in the wide and honest grey eyes. I can't live without you, Hugh darling! her heart pleaded in silent appeal.

The car and the picnic gear waited on the lower slopes just before the sleepy village. Neither had much appetite. Hugh turned and led the way along the path of hard orange soil, silently absorbed in the thoughts crowding his mind as he mulled over Liz's vehement protest. With the main obstacle now removed, was it such a preposterous idea after all? She'd never know how wrong she was about his emotions. Clearly she saw him as heartless, an automaton living for his work alone. Perhaps indeed he had been, until she came along. But she'd never know . . . not unless he told her how he really felt . . .

★   ★   ★

'Shan't be five minutes,' Hugh had said.

Liz glanced again at her watch, and peered from the car at the golden windows of the Clinic. It was well and truly dark. She didn't really want to seek Hugh out, not when she had already made her painful farewells to everyone there.

'I just want to leave this typing,' he'd said. And she'd watched his progress as the light flashed on in his office and he left his papers, then moved on down the corridors. He wasn't dressed for visiting patients.

Suddenly a shadowy figure in white materialised at Liz's elbow. It was Sister Cecilia. She smiled comfortingly at Liz in the grainy darkness, and the girl knew on the instant what the nun was going to say. 'The Little Flower?'

'Yes, dear. This afternoon. Very lovely it was, and peaceful. Now Mr Forsythe wants you to drive the car home and he'll come back by taxi. Shall you be all right to drive this great thing?'

Feeling extraordinarily tired, Liz went to her bed and slept right through till morning and the sound of Luisa sweeping outside her door. For a few seconds her mind stayed mercifully blank, then it all came rushing back — the picnic, where a lot of home truths were aired, bringing tension to an idyllic day. And the events that had kept Hugh late at the Clinic. Her flight home — that very afternoon.

There wasn't much to pack; it would take all of ten minutes. She must see to Hugh's breakfast first.

The kitchen looked as if a bomb had hit it. Hugh had clearly made himself a midnight snack, a Dagwood sandwich involving the entire contents of the fridge, just about every knife and plate in the cupboards and a snow of crumbs on the marble floor.

'No, no,' reproved Luisa when she found Liz on her knees with dustpan and brush.

Liz glanced up and smiled. 'Have you seen Mr Forsythe?' she asked. Luisa made swimming movements with both arms, then pointed cheerfully towards the garden.

'I think I'll join him,' said Liz incomprehensibly, and ran off to slip into a bikini. Just what was needed to douse the cobwebs and gauge Hugh's mood this morning. He was bound to be feeling very sad . . . and on her last day too.

She dived in and floated lazily on her back, letting the sun warm her face and toes as they stuck up out of the water. Waiting for Hugh to stop his marathon crawl and come and talk to her, if he felt so inclined.

'I'm so sorry,' she said with gentle warmth when Hugh materialised out of the greeny depths, at her side. 'You must have been very late getting back.'

'Hmm. Have any trouble with my car?'

Liz shook her head. 'Your usual breakfast?'

'Leave it another hour. I had a snack when I got in.'

'I did notice.'

He surged off towards the deep end, no mention of her imminent departure. Liz sighed and climbed the steps out of the pool. She'd better eat something herself since she must leave before lunch. It was up to Hugh to take care of his own needs from then on.

He seemed very much his old self over breakfast, frowning at the dish of peach jam Liz had set beside his plate and complaining because it wasn't marmalade. He just couldn't care less that I'm going, she mourned, tilting the sunshade to protect the butter.

'Marmalade was invented by the Scots, not the Portuguese,' she said.

'I can't be doing with this stuff,' muttered Hugh, shoving the dish away with a disdainful finger.

Liz couldn't resist a sly dig. 'Well, I could always bring you out a fresh supply of my mother's home-made marmalade. It's the kind you like best . . . ' His eyes gleamed. If he didn't want her, then he certainly liked the sound of her marmalade. The way to a man's heart! 'Thick . . . and dark . . . and chunky?'

'You bet!'

Hugh sprawled there in his wicker chair with the sunshine playing on his damp skin. But no positive reaction.

'This *stuff*, as you call it,' pointed out Liz tartly, 'consists of pure fruit and sugar and *no* additives. It's a crime to turn your nose up at good food.'

'Don't nag, woman. It's not what you're paid for.'

Liz flushed crimson. 'I wouldn't dream of accepting any payment, Hugh. This has been a fantastic holiday for me.' Understatement of the year, that.

A long arm shot across the table, and the pad of his middle finger probed the cleft of her chin. 'Don't tell me,' came the teasing drawl, 'you were toiling then for love?' Behind the black mirror-lensed sun-shades Hugh's eyes were specially watchful. With satisfaction he noted the tremor in her hands, the cups rattling in their saucers as she busied herself clearing the table. How could he possibly let her go? Yet it was now inevitable.

Liz swallowed hard, but kept her end up with a 'Love of sun and sand and sea,' and a brittle laugh that fooled no one. 'I have you to thank for my complete recovery. That's payment enough. You've been more kind and more considerate than I could have dreamed possible — ' She finished the sentence in her own head — for that beastly Mr Midnight-Blue I clashed with on the outward flight.

'You certainly do look the picture of health and beauty.' Hugh's eyes dwelled lovingly on the vision of Liz in her red polka-dot bikini, lissome and curved and golden, her hair hanging wetly down her back. He'd committed the fatal mistake — yes, it must be acknowledged as a fact — of enjoying her company too much. Her humour, her intelligence, her independent spirit. Her physical attractions only too evident. The whole package had added up to a fascinating total sum — and a dangerously complicated result.

A knob of butter slid off his toast and dropped on to his bare chest where it melted to a glistening oil, sliding down to the taut flatness of his stomach.

'Clumsy,' reproved Liz, passing across a tissue which Hugh made no attempt to take so that her fingers had to do the job for him, dabbing at the warm bronzed flesh with its springy coils of black hair. Obliged to lean close, Liz could feel Hugh's breath on her neck, his lips too close to her ear, the sly ironical murmur of, 'Thank you, Nurse — I feel much better now.'

His fingers stroked the flesh of her bare arm with butterfly tenderness. 'Do you realise I shall be thirty-four next birthday?'

'Could you move your elbow, please, Methuselah?'

'And you're what . . . twenty-one . . . two?'

'Uhuh.'

'Twelve years' difference.'

The jam spoon fell to the table with a clatter. Liz had stopped breathing several seconds back.

A hand closed over her wrist, forcing

her to put down the breakfast things, drawing her round to Hugh's side of the table, pulling her gently but inexorably into his lap — where it was perfectly natural for her arms to move up and wind about his neck.

'I ought to be packing,' Liz whispered as his mouth hovered over hers, cradled within the circle of his arms, flesh against flesh, that dark head blocking out the sun.

'We'd be more comfortable,' Hugh suggested huskily, 'on one of the sunbeds . . . '

Liz's last thought was a dizzy, So I'm about to become a fallen woman . . . who cares?

When at length they surfaced and she glanced at her watch with alarm, Hugh had a very practical suggestion all lined up. 'If I bring the diamond ring in three weeks' time — can you fix the marmalade, darling?'

'Reckon that's a fair swap, guv.' It was such a relief to let the blinds of pretence slip from her eyes and to look at Hugh and reveal all the love she had nurtured secretly for so long in her heart. 'And I know just how you like it best. Thick and dark and chunky . . . '

## THE END

We do hope that you have enjoyed reading this large print book.

Did you know that all of our titles are available for purchase?

We publish a wide range of high quality large print books including:
**Romances, Mysteries, Classics**
**General Fiction**
**Non Fiction and Westerns**

Special interest titles available in large print are:
**The Little Oxford Dictionary**
**Music Book, Song Book**
**Hymn Book, Service Book**

Also available from us courtesy of Oxford University Press:
**Young Readers' Dictionary**
**(large print edition)**
**Young Readers' Thesaurus**
**(large print edition)**

For further information or a free brochure, please contact us at:
**Ulverscroft Large Print Books Ltd.,**
**The Green, Bradgate Road, Anstey,**
**Leicester, LE7 7FU, England.**
**Tel:** (00 44) **0116 236 4325**
**Fax:** (00 44) **0116 234 0205**

*Other titles in the*
*Linford Romance Library:*

# FLAMES THAT MELT

## Angela Britnell

Tish Carlisle returns from Tennessee to clear out her late father's house in Cornwall — to several surprises. The first is the woman and baby she discovers living there and the second is her father's solicitor, Nico De Burgh, who was Tish's first love. Nico fights their renewed attraction because of a promise made to his foster father but Tish won't give up on him. They must share their secrets before they have any chance of a loving future together . . .